Aimee Ungersma is a single mother of two sons, Ian and Elliott. She works two jobs and writes in her spare time. Aimee's creative writing began in high school when she received extra credit on essays for entwining fictional stories with her history homework. Then many years later, she began to write her first book Damned If I Do, because she was at work telling tall stories and a co-worker told her that if she made that into a book, he would read it. So she wrote it! In her free time, she enjoys writing, playing outside with her sons, working out, trying to cook, and being around any kind of water. Aimee is looking forward to writing the next three books of the Damned Series for the readers.

I would like to dedicate and thank my friend Jim Fisher for encouraging me to write my book. To Marcia Stratton for inspiring me to make a character like you. To my sister Laurie and her husband Ryan for listening to my book and telling me when something sounded off. To Saundra, my brother Ronald, and my uncle Adam for editing. To my sons Ian and Elliott as well as my nieces Lorelei and Margot for your love. Lastly to Les and my other friends who helped me, inspired me, and believed in me.

Aimee Ungersma

DAMNED IF I DO

AUSTIN MACAULEY PUBLISHERS™
LONDON • CAMBRIDGE • NEW YORK • SHARJAH

Copyright © Aimee Ungersma 2022

The right of Aimee Ungersma to be identified as author of this work has been asserted by the author in accordance with section 77 and 78 of the Copyright, Designs and Patents Act 1988.

All rights reserved. No part of this publication may be reproduced, stored in a retrieval system, or transmitted in any form or by any means, electronic, mechanical, photocopying, recording, or otherwise, without the prior permission of the publishers.

Any person who commits any unauthorised act in relation to this publication may be liable to criminal prosecution and civil claims for damages.

This is a work of fiction. Names, characters, businesses, places, events, locales, and incidents are either the products of the author's imagination or used in a fictitious manner. Any resemblance to actual persons, living or dead, or actual events is purely coincidental.

A CIP catalogue record for this title is available from the British Library.

ISBN 9781398406094 (Paperback)
ISBN 9781398406100 (ePub e-book)

www.austinmacauley.com

First Published 2022
Austin Macauley Publishers Ltd®
1 Canada Square
Canary Wharf
London
E14 5AA

Thank you to Austin Macauley Publishers and their team for publishing my work. Thank you to Les, Amber, Dan, Ron, Margaret, Laurie, Ryan, Ronald and Adam for all of your help. Thank you to the Rohrman family, Riley, Mark, Jason, Marcel, June, Marilyn, and Jim as well as Cliff, Tina, and Courtney for your donations.

Prologue

I walked into the room, which reeked of coffee and wet clothes. Lightning flashed by the window, lighting up the raindrops pouring down outside. I looked to the middle of the room where six chairs had been placed into a circle facing each other. As I stared at the glum faces occupying five of those six chairs, the thunder followed the lightning with a loud clap that rattled the walls of the old building. This had caused my attention to go back to the window and let out a sigh.

As I stared out the window, I didn't hear the cough or the clearing of his throat, but when I heard, "uh, miss?" I turned my head to see an old man who was standing behind a woman sitting in one of the chairs. She had a bad acne breakout on her cheeks. He smiled at me but his eyes looked like he would rather have cut his own arm off then be here on a Thursday with the rest of us misfits. I smiled back at him as he asked in a kind but impatient tone, "Would you care to join the rest of us and share your name?" He indicated to the rest of the group with his hand.

"Oh shit, I forgot what I was doing for a second. Sorry." I laughed. While walking into the circle of chairs towards the empty one that was meant for me, I turned to face everyone and with a deep sigh (I do that a lot by the way). I stated proudly, "Hello, my name is Marcy Goode and I'm an alcoholic."

As I sat the whole group replied in unison, "Hi Marcy!"

Chapter One

That's right, I'm an alcoholic! Well not really, I don't like drinking actually. I just to go to the AA meetings because I like to hear other peoples' problems, to make sure their lives suck more than mine. does that make me a horrible person? Probably, but crashing the AA meetings on a Thursday night is a lot better than the time I tried to attend an anger management class. Those people had some serious issues, not to mention tempers that kind of scared me. Apparently, I didn't meet their criteria either but whatever, it's their loss. Not mine.

So what kind of problems could I possibly have in my life that would be bad enough that I would be willing to waste my time listening to the life story of a boozer you ask? Well, for starters, I am over three hundred years old. No, really. I was born during the Salem witch trials back in the late 1600s. My name is actually Mercy Good and like any other witch out there, I just age very slowly. Yes, you heard correctly, a witch.

I am the second child born to Sarah Good who was condemned and killed shortly after she gave birth to me during the witch trials. No, I am not immortal. I just age well like any other fine cheese, so I look like I'm only in my thirties. I should be dead I suppose, but my life was spared after I was born because a stranger approached my mother while she was in jail awaiting the gallows and offered to take my older sister away. My sister Dorcus (who later had her name changed to Dorothy) was also imprisoned for being a witch at just four years old. The stranger must have pitied my mother because I was saved too.

Snapping away from my thoughts and history I was back in the AA meeting. I let out a sigh as the instructor was still going on about how we were in the very middle of our twelve-step program. "Tonight is a very important night for us all," he went on in a monotone voice. "Step 6 of our program is surrendering yourself to God."

I cringed out in pain at his name and accidentally blurted out loud, "Oh shit." I began to panic, as everyone in the class looked in my direction with unhappy stares. I had been to enough of these things to know better than to come to step 6, I thought to myself, then turning a bit red in the face said, "Sorry," to everyone in the room. I quickly raised my hand causing the instructor to look surprised that I wanted to speak since the whole rest of the evening he all but had to pull teeth to get a word out of me.

"Yes? Um... I'm sorry I forgot your name, dear." He looked a little embarrassed that he didn't remember my name.

"Marcy," I replied, "I just realized that I left my purse at the liquor store and I really need to go get it before they close."

I'm pretty sure I just watched this man's eye twitch at my request but he said, "Of course."

I smiled while thinking to myself that I just broke this man's brain. "Thanks!" I said as I stood up, reaching for my purse, and hanging it over my shoulder. I had to squeeze myself between the chairs of people as I bolted for the door.

Yes, I realize that was a lame excuse but I had to get out of there like four minutes ago. Just as I was reaching for the door handle, it swung open to reveal a very tall man in a black wet coat and short brown hair. His beard was wet from the rain and dripping on the floor between us. He must not have seen me since I'm not the tallest crayon in the box because he was smiling at the rest of the class, however, just like the instructor, his smile didn't seem to reach his eyes either. What the hell, I thought to myself, am I the only one who actually enjoys coming to these things?

I went to walk past him when he reached out his hand and said in a very polite manner, "Good evening miss, I'm Father Shepherd." I looked up at him, then down to his outstretched hand, then back up to his face. He must have been six foot six the way he was towering over my five foot five frame. He still had his hand out waiting to shake mine.

I gave him the nicest smile I could manage and replied, "This is New York pal; we don't shake hands or touch other people here." His smile started to reach his hazel eyes as I could see his crow's feet start to appear. He nodded and put his hand down to his side.

I went around him to reach for the door handle when he asked in almost a concerned tone, "Is the class already over?" looking down at me then over to the instructor.

"Negative," I replied pointing to the circle o' fun. "They are still going."

I grabbed the handle this time before he turned his full attention to me, "Are you leaving?" I dropped my hand from the handle letting out a sigh before turning around to look up at him.

"Yes, I left my purse at the liquor store and I need to go get it."

He laughed for a moment before saying, "but your purse is right here, silly." He touched the strap of my purse that was resting on my shoulder. I swatted away at his hand, which went about as well as a kitten swatting at a tall piece of string. I glanced around him to see if the instructor had heard that and was quickly met with the glare of the old man. I groaned out then whispered to myself a very tasteful "son of a bisquick" as I stomped back to my chair in defeat.

The tall drink of water, who was now my enemy, walked over to the instructor where they shook hands and greeted one another. Oh sure, make a liar out of me, I thought looking at the instructor who turned to the class so he could introduce the stranger who foiled my escape plan.

"Everyone, this is Father Benjamin Shepherd, he will be the new priest at the Most Precious Blood Catholic Church here in town."

The room clapped for a moment then a member of the class asked, "What happened to Father Gabriel?"

The priest stopped smiling and replied in a saddened tone, "He passed away a few days ago." Many members of the class gasped in surprise. Hell, even I was a little shocked since he wasn't that old.

"He was murdered, wasn't he?" asked the instructor. Father Benjamin closed his eyes for a moment then nodded.

"We should say a prayer for him and his family?" stated a round lady sitting next to me wearing a sweater that looked as though it was made from cat hair.

"That's a wonderful idea, Connie!" replied the instructor looking up to the Priest for approval. Yeah, great idea Connie,

I thought shooting her a glare. The priest asked everyone in the circle to stand up and hold hands for prayer. I began to panic again as the priest smiled and held his hand out for mine for the second time tonight.

I was beginning to sweat as I felt like a cow who was about to visit the slaughterhouse. Now, I know what you're all thinking, but don't get all excited. I don't hiss or catch fire or anything like that. My ears just start ringing and I get a terrible headache. Everyone in the room was already joined hand in hand and it seemed like everyone was waiting on me. In that moment everything seemed to freeze as I unknowingly began to hold my breath while hoping that something, anything, would save me from this agony that was about to come my way. As though an answer to my plea, a bolt of lightning flashed brightly lighting up the room more than the fluorescent light bulbs and immediately the loud clap of thunder followed. It must have struck the building because the power went out and the walls rattled more aggressively this time. With the darkness in the room and everyone beginning to panic around me, I saw my window of opportunity, and by that I mean I saw my door of opportunity and I took it.

Within minutes I was walking down the sidewalk. My clothes beginning to soak up the tears from the sky. Normally, I would have a big smile on my face since I love the rain, but at the moment I just felt mentally drained and exhausted. I found a deserted alley where I collapsed against the wall. My heart was racing so hard I could hear my pulse. After a few moments, I let out a sigh of relief as I smoothed back my wet hair from my face. I looked up to the sky breathing in deep to relax myself. I was finding that this was hard to do since I felt as though I had just dodged a bullet. A "big holy bullet" named Benjamin.

Chapter Two

I'm not sure what time it was but on many nights like tonight, I have the same dream. I believe it's a dream anyway since I was not old enough when a few of these events occurred to be considered déjà vu. I am back in the town of Salem and I see the dark cloak of the person who took my sister and I from my mother and our possible deaths. I watched, as my mother seemed very grateful with such sadness in her eyes as she thanked the figure while holding me tightly to her. The cloak held her hand for a moment, after taking me from her and then we left into the night. A flash happened and the next thing I know, I am at my aunt Abby's house one hundred years later, which is where the kind stranger took us to be raised as nothing more than ordinary children. My aunt Abigail Larkum was a cruel woman with beautiful black hair that flowed down to her hips. It was the color of a crow's wings and her hateful eyes had the same color to match her hair. She was a heavyset woman who had never married or had children of her own. She did, however, have an even crueler cat named Burroughs. The damn thing didn't even like her, yet she kept him around to hiss, bite, and scratch at our arms or legs.

    In my dream, I was laying on my stomach at the top of the stairs listening as my aunt and sister Dorothy went toe-to-toe in a screaming match. "I will not have you or Marcy learning or doing any type of magic in this house, or while under my watch." My aunt shrieked, her face was red as she let her words ring throughout the room. I assumed the argument was over now since when it came to these fun times between them, she always had the last word.

I was about to stand up and head to my bedroom when I heard. "No, this is not over. I want to learn so I can see what I'm capable of." I froze in place glancing over the stair rail to see my sister taking a step towards our aunt as she continued on, "You can't keep who we are, shut away from the world and those who want to cause us harm." My sister's tone was so deep and quiet that I was having a hard time hearing but the tone in her was so threatening and full of hate that the hair on my arm began to stand up. I could see them facing each other, the light from the fireplace showing the glare in my sister's eyes as she went on. "If you won't teach us magic, then you are against us and I am old enough that I will leave this place and take Marcy with me."

I watched as my aunt struck Dorothy in the face. The slap sounded as though it was caused by a belt instead of her hand. I heard the thud as I watched my sister fall to the floor hitting her head against the table behind her. I almost made the mistake of going to help my sister until my aunt took a few steps forward now standing over my sister's limp body. She began to laugh as she reached down grabbing my sister up by her hair. This had pulled my sister's face up to look into hers. "Do not forget that I am the one who took you in at four and Marcy as a newborn. I did not have to keep either of you, yet I did. Magic is what caused us to run and hide from the people of the world and their cruelties." She finally released my sister, allowing her to drop back down to the ground. She turned away to look at the fireplace. After a moment of her watching the fire dance around, she said, "Your mother was killed because of magic, and yet you wish to learn the one thing that became our downfall, you stupid girl." My sister got herself up from the spot on the floor where my aunt had knocked her down. She was fighting back tears and still holding her cheek. With hatred in her eyes as tears started to fall down her face, she walked past my aunt and left the house for good.

I wake up wondering every night what happened to my sister. Did she find someone to teach her magic? Does she miss me at all like I miss her? Is she even still alive? My aunt Abby refused to talk about her, and when I would bring up her name my aunt would become furious and tell me to mind my business and change the subject. Life with my aunt was very hard for me while growing up. We had to move every so often to make sure no one noticed that we were not ageing at a normal rate. I was not allowed to play with any other children or be outside for more than twenty minutes. My aunt was on the edge of paranoia but would always assure me that it's what needs to be done. Finally, getting tired of moving around and even more tired of my aunt, I decided to move to a place where I could light a cop car on fire while dancing around it naked and no one would look my direction or even care. New York! Queens, New York, to be exact. This is where I opened my flower shop called "Stems of Hope" and I have lived here happily unnoticed ever since. Well, at least until the AA meeting from earlier.

While lying in bed, my mind began to race in that direction; and even more so in his direction. Why was he so damn tall, why was he so damn yummy looking, and why on earth did I get a warm feeling when the priest touched my shoulder. It was the feeling you get when you pull out a soft blanket fresh from the dryer and wrap yourself in it burrito style, while inhaling the old spice dryer sheet scent kind of way. Wait, what the hell I am thinking!? I sat straight up in my bed, like you would see in a horror movie. I could feel my eyes about to bulge from my head. This was the worst place for my mind to wander. I sat there trying to shake my thoughts from my head. No way should I ever think of a man of the church in a romantic way. I don't care how much of a sexy stack o' pancakes I thought he was. Nothing good could ever come from me imagining myself getting tangled with the cross. This pissed me off so much that I actually yelled at myself to go back to sleep. Insomnia is the worst thing, I swear.

I was running late to open up my store the next morning, not that it really mattered. I had very few orders due today and it's not like I have people lined up and down the block banging down my doors. It's mostly been the inheritance money from the trials that I use to keep my business going. I received the money one hundred years after the trials. It was given to immediate family members of any convicted and condemned witch. It's taken very good care of me throughout the years and anything I do sell from my business is just extra money.

Getting off the bus and power walking down the block just like old people do at the mall, I was now in sight of my beautiful store. I smiled seeing the green and black painted "Stems of Hope" sign hanging from above the French doors. My shop was a tiny brick building from the outside, but on the inside, it was large with hardwood floors. The ceiling, amazingly tall with beautifully sculptured lions positioned at the top corners of each wall like an old opera house. A large stained glass window of a woman receiving a rose from her love was placed above the French doors so perfectly that the colors would dance on the dark wood floors for many hours of the day. It made me feel as though I would actually have a good day for once. I grabbed my keys from my coat pocket, careful not to spill my coffee all over myself. I opened the door and reached down to grab the daily newspaper when my purse slid down from my non-existent shoulder and hit my hand. I almost spilled my coffee again, but no, a nice save made by Marcy (imaginary crowd goes wild). I smirked in victory knowing that today was my day. Or so I thought.

Chapter Three

I turned on the light in my shop and tossed my keys and purse on top of the desk that held the cash register. I was about to get my orders together when I looked down at the paper to see the front page reading, "Name of Local Priest Brutally Murdered Released." The image below the headline was the shadow of a man hanging from a tree. I sat down at my desk to open the paper and turn to the page instructed to read the article further. "Long time priest, Father Gabriel, of the Most Precious Blood Catholic Church was found dead Monday morning hanging from the oldest oak tree in the courtyard of the church. Suicide has been ruled out at this time. Drugs or alcohol do not seem to be a factor in the death. Father Gabriel was 58 years old and served the church for thirty-three years." I closed the paper, glancing at the picture on the front again. I can't believe the man died so tragically, young and alone, I thought to myself.

"Ouch!" I had finally lost my game to the coffee as it not only spilled down the front of my pretty red sweater but it also gave me a horrible burn on my hand. Damn it, I thought looking around on my desk for something to clean it up with. Letting out an angry sigh I grabbed some napkins to soak up the coffee on top of my desk before it reached my orders. I then walked over to the corner to get my black sweater out of my coat closet to put on. I'm so accident prone that I always keep back up clothes just in case. I pulled the coffee-stained sweater over my head when the door chimed to alert me that someone was entering the store. The February air filled the room and I could feel the cold brushing up my spine. You have got to be flipping kidding me, I thought as I realized my undershirt had also pulled up with my sweater. Just my damn luck, not only do I have a horrible coffee stain on my favorite sweater, but I also have a burn on my hand that hurts like a bitch, and now a complete stranger is staring at my black brassiere. I heard a hesitant footstep in my direction. "Don't!" I said loudly to make sure I was heard from inside my sweater. "Stay where you are, please. If you don't touch me I won't taze you." I managed to pull my undershirt down while still struggling with the sweater, wondering how on earth did a coffee spill cause my sweater to shrink so much that I can't even get it over my big ass head? "I don't suppose you have any butter on you to help me get out of this sweater, do ya?" I asked in a half-joking and half claustrophobic voice.

The footstep made a chuckle and a familiar voice said, "You do know that it unzips in the front, right?" I froze and as I unzipped my sweater to expose my face. There in front of me, who had just seen my black lacy bra was none other than Father Benjamin Shepherd. His smile got much bigger as he recognized that it was me.

I, on the other hand, managed to say, "Huh, I think I would have preferred a complete stranger." His smile backed off a little and his cheeks turned as red as my sweater pre-coffee. I instantly felt bad as soon as I realized he took that wrong. "Oh gosh, I'm sorry I didn't mean to say that out loud," I explained wishing that my brain would register what I was saying before I said it.

He looked at the floor with his cheeks still very red and said, "I am the one who is sorry. I should have excused myself when I saw you struggling. God forgive me." My ears suddenly rang so loud causing me to cringe in pain. He didn't notice still looking at the floor. "I can go outside if you need a few moments," he said in a very apologetic voice finally looking up at me.

I sighed in reply thinking, great, if I didn't already think I was going to hell, I really was going now. "It's fine," I said putting the black sweater on quickly. "What can I help you with?"

He made a step in my direction and ignoring my question asking his own. "Why did you leave the meeting last night?" Shit, I thought to myself. I was really hoping no one had noticed, especially him since he foiled my escape plan, to begin with.

"I had to leave because I was feeling sick." That wasn't a complete lie since I knew if I stayed at the meeting for the prayer I would have a headache from hell, so bad that it would cause me to throw up all night. And that, my friends, was definitely not on my list of things to do.

"Oh." His eyes scanned my face a bit concerned, "Well, I do hope you are feeling better this morning."

"Yeah, yeah, I'm fine. Now, for the second time today, what can I help you with?"

He suddenly looked like he had just aged forty years as his eyes saddened looking into mine. "I had ordered a funeral wreath for Father Gabriel, I was told it would be ready for pick up today." I just looked at him quietly wondering if I was to always be fated into looking like a jack-wagon every time I crossed paths with this man. He must have read my expression or thought I was mentally challenged because he asked again with a hint of a smile on his lips. "Is it ready?"

"Oh yes, yes!" I laughed at myself. I went to the walk-in cooler to retrieve the wreath. I walked back out to find him at the corner of my desk staring intently at my beautiful obese black and white colored rat named Ira. Yes, I take much pride in knowing that I own a fat rat. She can still walk though so I'm not a horrible pet parent if that's what you're thinking. She doesn't have to be rolled around. Yet.

"I have never been around someone who has had a pet rat before. May I pet her?" I couldn't tell if I was more surprised that he wanted to pet Ira or that he had never seen a tame rat before. I gently placed the wreath on the shepherds hook behind my desk and walked in the direction of Ira's cage.

I tried very hard not to breathe in his amazing scent as I approached him. He pulled his finger away from between the bars where he was petting Ira's face. Ira looked unhappy as she watched him step to the side to make room for me. I smirked at her sad face thinking to myself, yeah as though I don't give you enough love. Or food. I opened the cage door and scooped her up with two hands and a little of her chub spilled over the sides of my palms. I turned around to proudly present him with my prized piggy when he laughed. I looked at him wondering why the hell he was laughing at me. I looked down to see poor Ira wheezing as she attempted to walk out of my hands and into his. He gently rubbed her head with his fingers as she was still desperately trying to get to him. I guess I wasn't the only one who thought he was worth climbing on. That or he was hiding communion wafers in his coat. Shaking the dirty thoughts from my mind before it got to the dirty part, I set Ira on my shoulder where she hid behind my wavy brown hair. "Are you ready to check out?" I asked. He nodded then gently brushed my hair back from my shoulder to expose my rat that was at the moment attempting to bathe herself. He was so locked into the moment that he jumped a little as Ira sneezed. He laughed at himself looking away from Ira and locking his perfect hazel eyes with mine. His index finger moved a stray strand of my hair from my cheek to tuck behind my ear. His smile was so welcoming and kind that I didn't want it to end. However, when his hand touched my cheek something horrible happened.

It felt like I was in my dreams. There was a flash before me and I was in the pouring rain standing outside of the church. I heard muffled voices talking and felt terror in my stomach. I ran to the courtyard to see Ben tied to a stone table. Large rocks covered his body in a pile crushing him. There was blood coming from his head and mouth. He seemed very calm, as he spoke to the air, "You don't have to do this, my child, God can help you." I flinched in pain, then as almost to answer my question of who he was talking to, a shadowed figure in a cloak emerged from the shadows with a large stone hovering in the air behind it. I could not see the person just that the cloak was a very beautiful plum color, almost black and as it spoke, I knew it to be a woman. She hissed in a hurt and angry voice.

"God can help no one! Where was your God when we got unjustly accused without cause? Where was your God when families were ripped apart among the witches? Where is your God to help you now!?" The last question echoed throughout the courtyard as lightning struck through the sky to light up

Benjamin's pale face and his wounds. I could tell he was in pain and yet he still looked very calm. The large stone now lingered above him.

I held my breath as he closed his eyes and whispered, "Heal me, O Lord and I shall be healed; save me and I shall be saved for you are my praise."

"Stop it!" The cloaked figure screamed while covering her ears. She lost focus from the pain of Ben's words causing the final stone to drop.

"NO!" I screamed in horror as I was brought back to reality in my shop. His hand shot back to his chest as though it had been burnt by a hot kettle. My eyes went up to his, tears about to fall and I couldn't find my thoughts let alone get any words out. He was about to apologize for touching me when I put my hand up in a stopping motion. My body went into autopilot at that moment as I managed to go behind my desk to the shepherds hook and get the wreath. I held it out for him to take and as he grabbed it, I could see him reaching around for his wallet. I squeaked out, "Please leave, I... I don't want anything for it." He looked as though he was going to protest but the look on my face must have been enough. He nodded and looking ashamed of himself, left quickly into the cold.

Stunned, I stood there wondering what had I just witnessed. Ira must have sensed my anguish because she began to lick my cheek. I placed Ira gently in back into the cage and giving her my breakfast. Once she was safely off of me, I fell to my knees holding my hands in my lap. I stared up at the stained glass window finally letting my tears spill over as I looked up to the man giving his love a rose. My mind began to race faster and faster wondering if what I saw was going to happen. Should I tell or warn Ben? Would he even believe me if I told him? Was that just a daydream from my lack of sleep during the nights? Wiping my face, I stood up and knew I had to tell someone who might know what the hell that was, and I knew just the woman.

Chapter Four

"The slab of rock fell onto him and I came to before it crushed him and that was it. I was back in the shop with him," I said looking up at the ceiling trying to count the tiles. I was lying on a beautiful white Victorian-style chaise. My hands folded over my stomach. The smell of books and history filled the air. I went on with a sigh, "What do you think that means? Did I have like a daydream? Should I tell him what I saw? Should I be admitted to the funny farm?" I glanced over to a chair near my head where a beautiful woman who is my best friend, and also a fairy with short teased blond hair and green eyes, sat. Her black dress made her eyes stand out like a cat that spotted her prey. Her nails had a French manicure and her sandals were silver with beautiful gems that looked as though each gem was placed on very carefully.

Prudence Stafford has been my friend for a very, very long time. She grew up in a wealthy family but ran away from home back in the Eighteen Seventies to avoid an arranged marriage to a very wealthy and controlling man. She and I first met at "The Cat Call Saloon" in Wichita, Kansas. I had been working there as a server, giving the men of the Wild West their nightly round of beer, while dodging punches when fights broke out and beer glasses when they had too much to drink and became violent. I was about to quit and head back East since heading West with the gold rush was nothing but fights, death, and different men every night.

I had just got back to the bar to take a little break from the grabby hands of my customers when the owner and manager of the saloon, Phil, called me over to him. "Marcy, step behind the bar and fill as many glasses as you can while I head up to the stage for a minute." I nodded but let out a sigh of hatred as I watched him step up to the stage shouting for everyone's attention.

"Gentlemen, tonight's entertainment will be by the beautiful Prudence Stafford." The room got quiet as the curtain to the stage lifted to reveal a very tiny and short woman wearing a beautiful light blue sparkling dress. She held a matching fan in front of her face only exposing her piercing green eyes. Her beautiful blond hair was up in a curly ponytail that flowed down to the middle of her back.

The room was quiet as we all watched her, waiting to hear her sing. After a moment the piano started playing and she lowered her fan to her side as she began. Her voice was so magical sounding that my jaw dropped. I don't think anyone had ever heard a voice like that and her volume reached not only everyone in the saloon but by the time she finished her song, there were men in the doorways and even looking in through the windows to get a glance at the musical angel in the dress. Once finished, everyone lost their minds with applause and cheers. She took a bow, then gracefully bounced down the stage steps in my direction. I quickly caught her wrist and pulled her behind the bar with me because the men were starting to come over to get her attention.

"Thanks," she breathed, looking red in the face from her performance.

"You're welcome," I said letting go of her wrist. "My name is Marcy," I said handing out drinks as more people began to enter the saloon.

She smiled at me, "I'm Prudence but I'm thinking of changing my name to Pixie." I looked at her and repeated the name to make sure I heard her right. She nodded and then giggled, I couldn't help but laugh myself. We chatted for the majority of the night and even though I kept my distance from everyone, I really liked her as a person. She was very bright and kind but called it as it was, which I respected. Prudence went up to the stage for her second show of the night causing the same reaction from everyone as the first time. Once she was done singing, I got very busy with more requests for beer that I didn't even notice that she was missing until Phil came over to me where I was serving a table and asked if I had seen her anywhere. I glanced around the room and after a moment we heard a scream from the streets. Phil and I ran outside to see a very large man holding Prudence over the balcony of the saloon. He let go of her before anyone could try to talk him out of it.

As soon as she fell, Phil ran back in to get a hold of the man who just caused this poor woman's death. I, on the other hand, stood in the street and watched her fall at such a slow speed that I began to feel panic as I looked around into the faces of the other people standing near me watching the same thing. I knew most of the men watching were drunk and could easily be convinced that she died from the fall but not the few women that stood in the streets. I imminently took her hand as soon as she touched the ground (unharmed) and we ran behind the building. I heard shouting after us as I looked at her. "Are you a witch too?"

She looked at me stunned for a moment before answering, "No, I'm a Fay." We heard a whistle from the train behind the saloon as it was leaving. We made a jump onto the cart and finally allowed to breath, I looked at her.

"Fay, like a Fairy?" She nodded.

We ended up jumping train cars for a while until we were back on the East coast. We lived together, worked together, and traveled together for many years after that. Never had I met anyone I would rather spend my time around, like her. Even our fights were pathetic and we ended up talking the next day. Once we got in New York, I discovered my love for flowers and she discovered her love for her Crows and their findings. We, for the first time, split up and opened our own businesses and our own places. I would have been upset at this change had we not been so damn close. So, it all worked out for the better.

I heard a cough and it brought me out of my memories and back to the present time. I looked over to Prudence who was still in the same position as she was before I went into La- La- Land. She had been glancing at the newspaper with the headline reading a minister had been burned to death on a cross outside his church. It had a photo of the torched cross. She lowered her glasses then folded the paper neatly placing it on the table next to where she sat and glanced at me. Prudence sighed (about as well as I did) then said in an awkward almost an uncomfortable tone, "Honey, for the sixtieth time, you know I'm not a therapist, right?"

I threw my arm over my face and groaned out in misery,

"Well, why the hell not?"

She laughed and replied, "Because I got kicked out of college for having too many visitors. Speaking of, excuse me a moment." She stood up smoothing out the bottom of her dress and raised her arm up as though she were about to close line someone. Out of nowhere, a beautiful black raven landed on her outstretched arm and dropped an item into her hand. She looked at the item and said with a smile, "This should do just fine, Milos. Thank you, my darling." She stroked the bird's face and he took off. She came back to the chair and showed me a beautiful emerald ring. I rolled onto my side and propped myself up on an elbow as she handed me the ring to examine.

"What do you do if someone has insurance on something like that and you're found hocking it at an antique store?"

She smirked at me and replied with a know it all attitude. "That, my dear, is why I named the place Lost and Found Antiques." Then she stood up again and raised her arm up to get yet another bird who flew in from an opened window located at the front of her shop, which I'm guessing is where the first crow had come from. It gave her a paper rolled up around a wooden stem.

"Horace, for the last time please quit getting scrolls from other countries. They are very hard to sell and sit on the shelves gathering dust." She said to the crow, pointing in the direction of some ancient-looking scrolls. Then she laughed, "Well, I mean, they haven't been here since they were made so I guess it's not as bad as I'm making it out to be." She gave the bird a peck on its forehead and told it to just look for money or jewelry. With the new instructions, the bird was off. "Uh, Prudence can we please get back to my problem?"

She looked at me from the other side of the room. "Oh yes, of course, but you know I hate that name; that's why it's Pixie now." She went on, "Well, I'm not a therapist; I just play one on TV," she winked while grinning from ear to ear trying to cheer me up. Seeing that it didn't though, she let out a sigh and sat next to me where I was laying on the chaise. She scooped up my hands into hers and said as reassuringly as possible, "Look, honey, I'm not really sure what that was. Perhaps it's a power of yours since you don't know what yours are. It could be as you said it to be just a bad daydream. Or my third theory is that you are afraid to let your feelings for a man go anywhere." She paused as though she was debating if she should say the rest or not then continued. "Your mind is so traumatized from your aunt that the thought of another person in your life causes your cheese to slide off of its cracker and you flip out." She went on, "What I can tell you as your friend of almost one hundred and fifty years is that you shouldn't share this with anyone, especially the priest."

Just then the door opened and a tall muscular man stepped in. He unzipped his jacket, throwing into the chair that Pixie had sat in. He walked over, scooping her up in his arms, and planted a very large kiss on her mouth while sliding his massive hand up her leg to squeeze her thigh. She giggled as he lowered her to the ground trailing kisses on her neck. "Are you ready for our afternoon deligh…" He cut off noticing me for the first time since he entered and immediately corrected to "lunch date." I sat up from where I was laying feeling like I was intruding.

Pixie gave me a wink then told him in a sweet voice, "Rune, my love, give me five minutes and I will meet you at the Limo." He nodded kissing her hand. He picked his coat up from the chair putting it back on as he turned to leave. When he opened the door one of her crows flew in almost hitting

Rune in the face but he dodged it like a pro. I watched him as he now waited for her at the back of the limo with the driver.

She raised her arm out to accept the bird and it dropped something in her hand. She thanked Horace as he flew away and she looked at this item in her hand for a long moment. Ignoring her I asked, "Remind me again, how you managed to score a millionaire who is hotter than a movie star and waits on your hand and foot?" I went on looking at Rune, "He doesn't even mind your birds!" She finally looked up from the item at me and smiled.

"Well," she replied with a smug look on her face. "My birds are what caused him to come to my store. Milos took the money clip that his father had given him. So he followed him to my store where he and I haggled for a while on a price for the money clip," she continued while buttoning up her coat. "He was angry at first but when I wouldn't back down, even after he attempted his charm with me, he gave in with a laugh while fishing out fifty dollars from his wallet and told me he's never met a woman like me who can befriend the animals into robbing people. We talked for a while after that and he asked me out on a date. Here we are four years later," she said with a smile that made her look so beautiful. She began to walk to the door, eyes locked on her prince charming.

She stopped next to me and said, "Ya know, fate has a unique way to show you where love is." She dropped the item that she had been holding into my hands, kissed me on my cheek, and left the store. I glanced down at the item. It was a silver rosary.

I cursed under my breath closing my hand around the beads. Then realizing that I wasn't about to let her get the last words out on me all Dalai Lama style, I opened her shop doors and as she was getting into the limo, I shouted to her like any best friend would, "That's okay, Pixie; I'll just lock your store up for you." Bitch.

Chapter Five

I locked up Pixie's store and told her crows that they could have a lunch break, to which they squawked in my direction. I thought they understood me but then went and attacked the radio antenna on a parked car. I pulled my winter gloves out of my pocket and put them on. It was almost the beginning of March and if it wasn't raining then like today it was snowing. I walked glancing down at the rosary in my hands wondering why this man has been in town less than a week and yet I seem to see him everywhere I go? Why can't I run from this like everything else in my life? If anything I've become quite the pro at running when shit hits the fan. So why can't I run from him? "Oof," I ran into the back of a stranger standing at the Metro entrance. He was looking at the women going up the stairs while on his phone when I walked into the back of him. "I'm sorry; I wasn't paying attention to where I was going."

He spun around and said, "It's alright, my dear Marcy." My heart instantly fell into my stomach.

There, in front of me, stood my Landlord, Cleatus. He was a man that would make a snake's skin crawl. He was five foot nothing and round in all the wrong places. He wore gold plated jewelry that turned his skin green. He tried to intimidate others by making himself come off as a mob boss.

But I knew he was nothing more than a perv with his mommy's money. "I'm just heading back to your place actually, would you like to join me?" he asked in a seductive way that caused me to throw up in my mouth.

"No, I'm okay, thanks," I replied taking a huge step away from him. "I have to head back to my store to get some lastminute orders finished." This wasn't a complete lie. I was going back to my store but to mostly think more about what Pixie said, while working.

"Oh honey, I insist you let me get you there. It's such a dangerous part of town we are in." He grabbed my wrist and began to pull me in his direction and I was about to tell him to go pound sand when I glanced up only to lock eyes with none other than Father Benjamin who was across the street with a bag of groceries in his hands. He looked from me to Cleatus who was still holding my wrist with one hand and sliding his second one under the back of my coat towards my ass. He gave it a good squeeze causing me to squawk in surprise. Before I could say anything, Ben stood before both of us. How he got to us so quickly, I have no idea. He was looking down eyeing the baldhead of Cleatus and I swear I saw hatred in his eyes. He, then, shifted his gaze to me. Looking at my facial expression for clarification on if I needed help or not.

Cleatus looked displeased as he asked Ben, "Do you need something, pal, because we're busy." he asked as he gave me another squeeze. I was so busy trying to pull myself from his grip that I didn't see Ben clenching his fist as though he was going to strike Cleatus.

By the time I looked up at him, Ben just calmly looked at me again and said, "I need this young lady to show me the way back to her store. I had to stop and get money to pay her for a job she has done for me today." Cleatus looked at me and I avoided his stare as Ben went on. "It seems I have lost my way and am very relieved to have run into the two of you so I can get back there again." This time, I met my landlord's look and he let me go. Ben held his hand out for mine and after a brief moment of us looking at one another, I simply strode past him in the snow. As I walked away, I heard Ben thank Cleatus for his time and begin to follow closely behind me. He was so damn tall that in no time at all he was already at my side walking with me.

We walked this way for a while. Then finally, I said quietly, "Thank you."

He knew what I was thanking him for and replied, "Yes ma'am." Then after a moment, he asked, "Who was that guy anyway?" I sighed having to think about Cleatus again.

It gave me chills as I replied, "He is my landlord."

We stopped at a crosswalk and he turned to me worried. "Does he grab all of the tenants that way?"

"Negative," I replied as the light changed for the pedestrians to cross the road, "I'm just the lucky one."

He was quiet for a moment then looked at me quite seriously and said, "I hope you are joking." This had caused me to smile for the first time today.

"Yes, I was being sarcastic."

He thought for a moment then chuckled as he said, "You are good with sarcasm."

We rounded the corner to see my shop at the end of the block when I slid on a patch of black ice. Before I could register what was happening, Ben's hand wrapped around my waist in order to prevent me from kissing the sidewalk. This had caused his groceries to smash between our two bodies. He didn't even seem to notice as he looked into my face with concern. "Are you alright?" he asked as he attempted to stand me up straight.

"Yes, I think I'm okay." I wiggled out of his grip. I took a step and realized my ankle wasn't agreeing with my statement.

I tried my best to walk without any pain coming across my face but I think he knew it because he said gently to me, "If you'd let me, I can help you."

I rolled my shoulder as a boxer would, "Nah, I'm good." I replied but I almost fell over from the pain shooting through my ankle and for the second time he caught me. Without warning he put his arm under the back my coat but instead of grabbing me like Cleatus did he simply gripped my side, crouched down to my level, and slung my arm over his neck. He walked beside me using his weight to carry mine the rest of the way to my shop.

I unlocked the door to my store and he turned the light on. Once he helped me sit on my couch in the back, he asked me while removing my boots if I had an ice pack anywhere, "It's too damn cold for that don't ya think?" I replied in a sarcastic tone then immediately apologized for cursing around him.

He smiled and said, "No, it's alright. Give me a moment and I'll be right back." He stood up towering over me then bent down on one knee again to put my ankle on top of a pillow and then getting my second leg up onto the couch to put me in a more comfortable position. He disappeared to the bathroom and I lay there for a moment almost enjoying the fact that he was, in a way, taking care of me. Then my aunt's words rang in my head to never let anyone close to you especially someone who is not one of us. My happiness faded as fear and anxiety swept over me.

After a moment he emerged from the restroom with a hot washcloth. "I didn't realize how large this building was on the inside." I tried to reach out and grab the washcloth but he pulled it away from me.

"My landlord's mom gave me an amazing deal on the building and it gave me so much room for the flowers and the walk-in cooler," I said as he placed the washcloth on my sore ankle gently sitting at the opposite end of the couch from me. "I can do this, Father Benjamin; you don't have to stay here with me." I reached for the cloth for a second time and he looked at me with a stern look that was kind. I don't know how the hell he managed to do that but it was quite a trick.

"I want to stay here with you since you were hurt while with me," he said, "Also, it's just Ben when I'm not at church."

He lifted my leg a little to remove the pillow from under it and placed it behind my back for more support, then he placed my swollen ankle on top of his lap. It was so nice to sit there and stare at him but I was still panicking. I looked at the clock, "It's getting late, don't you have some priest stuff to do?" I asked in a hurry. He ignored my question and he sat there with his head bowed and eyes shut as though he was asleep. "Won't your groceries spoil?"

His eyes still shut but the corner of his mouth turned up into smiled, "My groceries are not going to spoil and I smashed them anyway when I saw you were about to fall." "Now let me finish my prayer for you, please." He said, then his mouth dropped into its original state.

His prayer seemed to take an eternity and finally, he looked up at me. His eyes locked with mine for a moment then he looked down at my coat pocket. "My Rosary!" he said with such delight in his voice. "I must have dropped it when I was in here this morning." I pulled it out of my pocket and reached over to place it in his waiting hands. "Thank you, Marcy." At that moment his hands held mine. Warmth filled my entire body from head to toe. The way he smiled at me made my heart dance and in this moment, I felt the happiest I had ever felt in my entire life. Then darkness swept over me. I was gone and it was cold. It was happening again.

Chapter Six

The flash, the rain, the voices, and the Church. It was all there exactly as it was before. It registered to me that it was happening exactly as it had, and it would surely end as it had the first time. I was prepared this time and I couldn't let him die, I just couldn't. Not wasting a moment, I ran around the church going in a different direction to enter the church courtyard. The cloaked woman buried him with stones. I could hear his bones crushing and breaking.

I looked around frantically, unsure of what to do. The only thing around me was a large branch from a tree. It must have fallen when the tree was struck with lightning. I grabbed it and moved in for my target. I felt like I was moving in slow motion and it angered me greatly because every second was needed to save Ben. As I approached, I kicked a small rock and it rolled toward the woman in the plum cloak. "Not a step further, Marcy." She then raised her hand and the rock I kicked, levitated into the air and then in a flash it hit Ben in his leg. It was at such a rate that it pierced his thigh causing it to bleed, and him, to roar in pain. I froze in place now knowing that she meant business and she also knew my name.

"Why are you hurting him?" She turned to me and I saw her face. Long and thin with her cheeks caved in as though she had never seen food a day in her life. Her eyes were as black as a dark hole. Her skin was so pale that she was almost transparent. I felt sorry for her as she had a crazy look on her face.

"This man believes that my soul can be saved if I surrender to God." She and I flinched and she went on, "Who is God to tell me that I need to be saved?" We flinched again in pain as she said His name again. Meeting my gaze she laughed a laugh that would make you feel uncomfortable as walking down the hallway at a psych ward.

"I know you don't need anyone to save yourself." I stood up trying to look as tall as possible as I continued, "But let him go please, he has done nothing wrong."

I hated myself for begging an unstable monster but the more time that went on the more I could feel Ben slipping away to the light. "See, my dear, that is the difference between you and I," she said with an evil smile on her thin face. "I don't take pity on anyone. I listen to no one. And I sure as hell don't give in to anyone." As she said the last part, she raised the final stone from the first time that was meant for Ben. However, unlike the first vision I had, she moved the stone from him to me.

I took a step back and realized I had backed up to the wall of the church. Fear fell on me. As the stone was flung in my direction all I could think was, this is it. This is how I was going to die. The stone hit me and everything was dark. They say in medical classes that your hearing is the last thing to go as you die. Well, I can tell you, I wish it wasn't because I heard Ben yelling my name in panic and her scary laughter mere moments before I heard my own skull crushing.
Everything went black and then there was light.

Chapter Seven

I came out of it sweating. There was a cold washcloth on my head. I had a blanket covering me and as I tried to kick it off a hand shot out from the dark to stop me. Not realizing someone else was with me in the room I jumped and screamed. "Shh. Marcy, it's me, Ben." I stopped screaming but my heart was still beating at two hundred miles an hour. A wave of nausea fell over me instantly and he must have seen it in my face because he quickly grabbed the bucket sitting on the floor near my head and put it in front of me. I got sick then, he reached around me and grabbed the glass of water from the side table and handed it to me.

"Thank you," I croaked as I took a swig of the water and spit it into the bucket.

He turned the lamp on at the other end of the couch where he was still sitting with my leg in his lap. He carefully examined my ankle. "The swelling in your ankle is almost gone, so that's good." He looked at me, worried. "However, you got a fever almost as soon as you laid down. I'm worried." He went on, still preventing me from kicking the blanket off of my body. "You would mumble that your head was killing you, get sick, and then fall back asleep."

I looked at him, so tired that I felt the room fading away from me again. I managed to mumble out, "I get very bad headaches, Doctor Ben."

He chuckled, "I am not a doctor, though I was a Corpsman for the Navy a few years before I joined the church." Then he got serious again. "You could have caught some type of bug."

I watched him through half-closed eyes as he continued thinking out loud. "That would be the most probable cause for your illness. It's not normal for someone to throw up that much with just a headache."

"Oh yeah, that reminds me," I said and sat up. He helped me sit up and looked as if he was going to ask what he reminded me of. I sighed for a moment miserably cutting off any question from him only to turn my head and barf. I groaned as I felt like I had nothing left in me to come up. I began to cry and asked him around my sobs. "You said you were in the military. Can't you kill me or something and make this stop?"

He chuckled as he wrapped me up in his arms moving my hair to the side and rubbing my back. "A Corpsman is a medic so even during that time in my life, I didn't kill people. I only tried to heal them." This felt amazing and he smelled delicious. "Also," he whispered in my ear, "You can't ask a priest to kill you because it's a sin."

I gave a half-ass chuckle and replied, "Well, that's no Bueno," and fell asleep.

I awoke to the noise of Ira chewing the bars of her cage. That was the strangest dream I think I have ever had, I thought sitting up from the couch only to see Ben sitting in a slouched position where I was just lying. I couldn't help but smile. It wasn't a dream. He took care of and held me as I slept in his arms. My heart did a dance then because life hates me, my brain registered what had happened and kicked my heart in the head. "Oh, crap," I whispered so as to not wake him (because I'm not a complete ass, ya know.)

I pulled myself from out of his arms and made my way to the bathroom feeling my head spinning. Oh, this was bad, Marcy I thought closing the door to the bathroom and running water on my face. What did I do? He is a priest for crying out loud and you wake up sleeping next to him!? I felt like I was going to cry as my thoughts raced on like a pissed off parent questioning a child. Hell for all you know from his practiced beliefs you two are married or worse you took his priest virginity away from him. Then regret set in as I questioned my honor as a good person. Oh gosh, he is married to the church and I fell asleep in his arms. Am I now a home-wrecker, or worse a hussy??? What will happen to him because of this, will I get him kicked out of his church for that?

I looked up at myself in the mirror with all of these questions flying around in my head and to add salt to the wound, I had the worst case of bed-head ever. "Oh, double crap," I said frantically trying to figure out what to do. I don't keep a hairbrush here. Hell, you're lucky if I remember to wear underwear when I leave the house. I didn't even have a hair tie to put my hair up in some sort of messy bun. I was hosed. I groaned sliding down the wall to the floor.

I put my head on my knees thinking how this could possibly get any worse. When I heard a faint knock on the door, "Marcy, are you okay?" Since I knew that wasn't my rat, Ira, I sighed knowing it did just get worse because Ben was now awake.

Lifting my head from my knees, I answered, "I'm okay." I could hear a sigh of relief from him on the other side of the door. "Do you need help with anything?" he asked still a little worried. "No. I'm fine, thank you, Father Benjamin." He was quiet for a moment. So I went on knowing he was taken a bit back from my formality with his name. "I am perfectly fine. You can leave, Father. Thank you so much for helping me." I could still see his shadow and I held my breath waiting for him to move or do something.

"Did I do something wrong, Marcy?" he finally managed. I could hear the hurt and confusion in his voice because it's the same hurt and confusion I could feel in my heart.

Not knowing what else to say because I didn't want to sound like a fool I just said, "Not at all, I just need to get ready to open up my shop."

I remembered his groceries are smashed and probably ruined from helping me. "Father Benjamin, if you push the green button on the cash register you can take fifty dollars out of it to get yourself more groceries." I didn't hear an answer. "Father Benjamin?" I wondered if he left but I didn't hear the bell for the front door go off.

Finally, I heard him say, "That is very kind, thank you." And after a moment I heard the bell from the door and let myself out of the bathroom. I walked over to my desk to give Ira some cereal and fill up her water bottle. I glanced down at the register to see a note. "I do hope you feel better, I can't accept your money but thank you anyway. Also, I am sorry if I did something wrong." Signed, "Ben." I opened the register to see that he indeed didn't accept my money.

I sighed cursing myself. Why on earth does everything in my life fall apart? It seems when I'm trying to be helpful, that's when it blows up in my face. A tear fell onto the note Ben had left me and I put it in my register. Was Pixie right? Am I self-destructing any kind of contact I have with good people for the fears my aunt smashed into my brain? Could I ever let anyone into my life as she did? I asked myself this while putting my coat on to head home for a shower and some food. I sighed passing the mirror on the wall next to the Lilly section in my shop, glancing into the mirror I laughed and said out loud to myself, "Not with your hair looking like that, honey!"

Chapter Eight

My day at the shop seemed to drag on with no mercy. I sat wondering if I should just close up and go home. No one wants to order flowers in a blizzard. Sighing I let my thoughts wander as I sat at the desk watching Ira waddle around on it. I felt so tired but I slept so well once my sickness was gone. I wonder if Ben slept well at all taking care of me. Should I send him a thank you card? No, that could get him questioned by the church if he got a letter saying, "Thanks for last night (wink)." I chuckled, thinking I would be an ass like that if he weren't a priest. Then, as thinking how well I actually slept, I realized that for the first time in years, I didn't have my dream. I sat up startling poor Ira who ended up rolling over from her weight. I felt awful scaring her, so as soon as I straightened her back up onto her feet, I stroked her cheek with my finger.

"I can't believe I actually slept without my dream," I thought out loud leaning forward in my chair to lay my head on the desk. "It felt great not to have it, don't get me wrong. But what does it mean?" I said to Ira as she chewed on a potato chip I gave her. "Was I just so drained from being sick that my dream just didn't happen?" Ira sneezed in reply. I wiped the wet area on my cheek. "You could be on to something my rodent!" I smiled at her and went on like a crazy person talking to my pet as though we could understand one another. "I should go to Salem tomorrow and pay a visit to Tituba. She was the most well-known witch during the Salem witch trials because she was the first to confess to being a witch and lived." This would help me so much if she were the real deal, I thought to myself while standing up from my desk. "Since Pixie couldn't tell me that I'm insane, maybe Tituba can!" I yelled in delight to the empty room feeling as though I could finally get some much-needed answers. I scooped Ira up into my hands and spun in a circle. Ira squeaked in anguish watching her half-eaten potato chip fall to the desk. I put her in her cage thanking her for her advice. "You are so amazing, Ira. I don't care what everyone else says." I kissed her little pink nose through the bars and she bit my lip in return. "Ouch, jerk." Then I realized her food bowl was empty so I gathered some cereal and on my way to return it to her cage, saw her potato chip. I placed it on top of her food bowl like a chef putting the finishing look on a very expensive dish. "We are going to talk about your attitude when I get home, lady."

The five-hour drive from Queens to Salem was very calming. I love the flow of New York, don't get me wrong. Like a leopard in tall grass, my existence is perfectly camouflaged by the tall buildings, the fast pace of day to day, and of course the aggression and lack of caring by the people. However, I needed this for many reasons. The first being that I needed answers that no one else that knows of what I truly am can give me. Two, I have always been curious about the place I was born in. All the moving we did growing up, my aunt Abby avoided Salem and Massachusetts like the plague. The third reason is I needed to get away from the priest who is turning my life right side up. It seemed the more he helped me, the more harm came to him. I may be a witch but I am not a cruel person. Seeing him hurt and sad tears me down to my core. So I figure, the further away from him I am, the happier and more importantly, safer he will be.

I reached Salem before 8 pm and got a hotel for the night. I had never met the infamous Tituba before so while at the hotel, I figured I could look up any information about her to help me know what to do and how to approach her. I have been told that she is legit as a witch but I don't know what her powers are or what strength she holds over the witch community. After a few hours sorting through possible facts about her being the slave to the girls who were the main accusers of the Salem witch trials, I got to know that she was also one of the first accused witches during the trials. There was also a lot of BS including a Facebook page which looked like medieval cosplay. I just gave up and decided I should go downstairs to the vending machine since I didn't stop to get dinner. I got some ones from my purse and knowing that the vending machine wasn't but twenty steps down the hall, I left in my very black and very short nightshirt that read, "If you're happy and you know it, it's your meds!" "Shake" "Shake" was written on each side of a pill bottle picture just below the song. Yes, that was special ordered, thank you for asking.

I located the glorious vending machine and decided on strawberry pop tarts for my night snack. Skipping down the hall I reached my door with half a pop tart hanging from my mouth when I realized I didn't have my room key with me. I was so quesoed as I stared at the door hoping it would see my anger and just open. I stuffed the rest of my snack in my mouth then began to jiggle the door handle frantically (but quietly at the same time so I didn't attract attention to my halfnaked self.) Really, it's my own fault though; when I ordered this awesome nightshirt, I laughed out loud when they asked me if I wanted to add pockets to the shirt for ten extra dollars. My cheap ass thought why on earth would you need pockets on a nightshirt and declined. "Well, this is gonna be awkward," I said to myself as I walked in the direction of the lobby holding my nightshirt down to cover as much of myself as possible.

There wasn't a soul in sight, which was good because no one got to see my clothes or lack thereof. However, it was just as bad since there wasn't anyone at the front desk. I groaned as I walked back to my room wondering how the hell I am going to get back into it. I stood in front of my door then it came to me. I'm a witch for crying out loud. Maybe I can say some spell and get it to open for me. It works in the movies. I stood back and while pointing at the door said, "Open, please." I waited and nothing happened. I wiggled my nose while thinking of the door opening and all that happened was I sneezed . "Damnit," I said. "Okay Marcy, you got this." I figured giving myself a pep talk could help.

I was in the middle of bouncing my head I dream of Jeanie style when I heard, "Marcy? Marcy Good?" I turned my head to see Riley Vanderwall walking in my direction.

I looked back at the door and said with a pleading almost threat in my tone, "If you love me at all, you'll open up right now!" It didn't.

"Riley," I said as though I didn't recognize him. He smiled his million-dollar smile at me as he approached. I was hoping after nine years he would forget about me. But alas, that was a negative as he picked me up for a hug. I arched my back to reach the bottom of my nightshirt to hold it down. He lowered me to the floor and said in such a happy tone it made me feel bad to not feel the same way.

"You look amazing!" he said looking me up and down. "You haven't changed one bit."

"Oh yeah," I chuckled nervously. "Ya know me I like to keep everything looking the same." I leaned on the door with my hand on the doorknob desperately trying to get it open as Riley went on.

"I can see that," he said. "So listen, I'm sure you are not in town long but I really haven't forgotten about you since we went out those couple of times when we were in college." Yeah, no shit, Sherlock, I thought as he continued on. "I still don't know what happened between us, Marcy."

He said my name to get my attention to him and off of what was in my head at the moment. "We had a great time together on our dates. I felt like we could have gone places together and then you ghosted me." He said the last words in a confused tone. I looked at him and not knowing what to say, decided to do what I do best and pull it out of my ass instead.

"Riley, my dear, ghosting is such a strong word." Yeah, that's it keep going I thought to myself. "I just felt like you didn't want me and instead of letting my heartbreak over a great guy like you." Oh nice one! I thought again. Yes, I really do have conversations like this in my head. Also, this wasn't a lie because Riley was a great guy with the nicest ass around. No joke! Unfortunatley he was too pretty and he didn't like the same things I liked, so yeah, I may or may not have ghosted him. "I just moved away before I became brokenhearted over you, Riley." As I said his name I fell into my room. I sat up thankful that the damn door finally opened only to realize that it was still shut and now I was in my room. I stood up and opened the door to see Riley gone faster than pancakes on a Sunday. I was so confused on how I managed to fall through the door. I decided after a moment that I did get what I wanted which was to get into my room so with a shrug I said, "meh." I'll just add that to my list of questions for tomorrow. I walked to the bed and crashed.

Chapter Nine

My dream was one for the books that night. I was walking to the town of Salem but before I could enter the town, they needed me to get on a large scale. It was so random but hell I just figured it was like a bridge law kind of thing where the town could only hold so much weight. I had to empty my pockets as the teenage girl in front of me went up to the scale. They measured her height and said she should weigh more than one hundred lbs. They put the weights on the other scale and she did indeed weigh more than one hundred pounds. She was given a certificate and continued into the town.

My turn came up and I stepped on the scale. They measured me and said I should weigh more than one hundred and sixty pounds. They put the weights on and I went up instead of the pounds. Cool, I thought, I did not want to be overweight. Just then I was arrested with men screaming, "Witch," in my face. I was immediately brought into the town where I was about to meet my end. My aunt Abby was in the crowd and said as I walked by. "I told you and your sister that magic was what caused our downfall. Now you will die like your mother for it."

I tried to tell her that I didn't even do any magic when a woman stepped in between my aunt Abby and I. Her voice was wise with age and stern as she looked at my aunt and said in a demanding voice, "You need to leave this child's dreams alone. You are a monster to cause Mercy so much pain in the one place she can escape the world and be in peace." My aunt glared daggers at her then looked at me and vanished. So did everyone else, but the kind stranger and I were left in the town. She turned to me and said, "Your dreams will no longer be controlled by that woman, Mercy." I thought I had heard her wrong the first time but I definitely heard my actual name again.

Afraid of my birth name being known by anyone, I quickly corrected her, "My name is Marcy."

She gave me a tired smile and said, "I know." I woke up a bit frightened. I pulled my knees up to my chest wondering if coming here was a mistake. Maybe being here brought back things that I don't want brought back. I got up getting myself a drink of water then lying down.

"Please, don't let me have bad dreams." I pleaded out loud to the room as I drifted back to sleep.

I awoke to the sun coming through the window of my room. I awoke feeling safe and surprisingly energized. I took a shower and packed my things for my 11 am check out. I headed downstairs for the complimentary breakfast. When I walked past the front desk and overheard a familiar voice shouting at the manager. "I'm telling you what I saw!" I saw Riley waving his arms all over the place like a chicken with its head cut off. "This place is haunted and I didn't sleep at all last night so I want my money back!" I smirked hearing the panic in his voice. I walked towards the dining area watching him. Perfect timing happened just as he turned his head in my direction I smiled and vanished into the dining room. He must not have known the dining area was an open room because I heard a scream of terror from him, "See what I mean!" Then the manager was telling him to calm down.

Laughing I grabbed some toast and scrambled eggs for breakfast. I grabbed a bottle of ketchup to make myself a quick but yummy egg sandwich (don't judge). I sat there eating as I glanced up from my table to see some chickens and children running around outside. I smiled at their cuteness, and then I saw her pass by the window exactly as she looked in my dream. I almost choked on my food wondering if that was really her. I got up in a hurry almost tripping over a chair to ask a girl who was collecting dishes from the tables. "Excuse me, but who is she?" I asked while pointing to the woman standing outside.

"Her? Oh, that's Janeka. She works here in the town as the slave witch Tituba." I could feel my heart drop as what I was being told sunk in.

"She isn't the real Tituba?" I asked in a defeated voice.

The girl giggled, "Heavens no, honey, the trials were like back in the 1690s." I cringed as she said Heaven, then laughed with her so as to not sound like a complete fool. She went to another table and I just stood there looking out of the window wondering why I thought this would be a good idea. I glanced over to where she was feeding the chickens and watching the children run around when her eyes locked with mine. I froze wondering if she was looking at me or if she was just zoned out like I do sometimes. I moved and her eyes followed me. She smiled and nodded at me.

I can't explain it but I could feel something from her. As though I should go talk to her anyway. I debated for a moment while putting on my coat and walking outside. She was walking into the jail and I decided it's now or never, Marcy, as I followed close behind her. When we entered, she turned the light on and I held my breath as I took in the sights. Was this the same jail that my mother had me in? I wondered feeling the bars. "Yes, it is." The woman replied pointing to a specific cell in the jail causing my heart to jump into my throat from terror. Did she read my mind just now or my face? I asked myself this while trying to keep my face as blank as possible and make my heart go back where it's supposed to be. "I can only read minds," she said with a mischievous smile, "Well, that and walk in dreams." I looked at her and with tears beginning to fall I asked in a broken tone, "You're not Janeka, are you?" She laughed while shaking her head. "No. I am Tituba the one you seek to answer your questions." She pulled me in for a hug and I let her.

I'm guessing I was in shock since I was unable to move or feel my body at all. She grabbed my hand and led me in the direction she was going. Turning on the lights to the rest of the jail, she stopped at a few cells and kicked the doors. "Time to get up, my witches." I looked into the bars at the piles of straw only to see they were women lying under the straw and when they sat up, I could see their clothes were torn. Their faces were filthy from lack of showering. They saw me and instantly began to sob and plead to me to release them.

"Please, help us. We are not witches. We are being held here against our wills. Free us, please!" One grabbed my shirt and Tituba hit her hand with a willow branch she was holding. The branch caused a loud cracking noise and the girl shrieked out in pain. The other two girls instantly backed away from the bars where they were also reaching out for me to save them.

The shock left me as I began to feel fear. Does she keep everyone who finds her and lock them away like this? Will I be the newest person for people to walk by and think is acting when I'm really being held prisoner? "No, Mercy," she stopped when she saw my face still full of fear. "Marcy." I looked at her. "You do not know of the things these demons have caused. I do not imprison the innocent. These girls are the very ones who imprisoned many of us a long time ago, including your own mother and sister." I guess I wasn't following very well because she pointed to the bars and said, "Before you, are Elizabeth or better known as Betty Paris, her cousin Abigail Williams, and Ann Putnam the girls who caused the Salem witch trials."

I looked from the pale faces of the women in the jail cells to Tituba. "How are they even still alive? Would they not have passed a long time ago?"

She looked at me and replied, "They would, but they age slowly like the rest of us." I looked at Tituba, waiting for her to laugh like she was kidding but no emotions came, except for her stern look.

I couldn't think of anything to say but, "Oh hell no!"

She nodded at me and while pointing at the girls again confirmed what I was thinking. "These girls are witches themselves."

I turned to them so angry screaming, "How could you!? What the hell is wrong with you people?" I could feel the rage in me and I didn't want to keep it in anymore. All of my problems, my worries my miserable life was now their fault.

I reached the bar when a hand grabbed my shoulder.

"Marcy, don't! I know you are hurt now but I have made it my life's work to ensure that these monsters have suffered since the trials have ended."

I backed off still feeling betrayed somehow. "How do they not get out?" I asked glaring at them.

Tituba grabbed my hand again and said, "Not here. Come with me and I will explain and answer your questions so you can go home." I followed her toward a mansion that read, "Paris Mansion." We went inside of a small house located behind the mansion that was known as the servant's quarters, as we entered, Tituba ushered me to a table where there was a small fire burning in the middle. She made us tea and sat across from where I was. "Now," she said with a smile. "Where would you like to start?"

I asked almost before she finished speaking. "How do they not get out of the jail?"

She set her tea down as she replied, "I have a curse put on the bars. They do not know how to break it."

I shot out another question almost instantly, "How has no one realized that you don't age, or them, for that matter?"

She smiled. "I have my granddaughters visit me every so often and apply for my position. Then I go under their names. And the girls in the jail, well, we just tell people that it's simply makeup and a wig on different girls." I sat back for a moment. "Anything else?" Tituba asked as I thought for a moment.

"Was my mom in pain when she died? Why didn't any witches fight?"

She looked sad as she replied. "My dear, most of the accused and condemned were not witches. Honestly, not all of the girls who did the accusing were witches," she indicated pointing to a heart in a jar on her coffee table.

I felt like I was going to throw up my toast, eggs, and possibly my pop tart from last night. "Tituba, who the hell's heart is that," I asked as I could feel all of the blood leaving my face.

"It belongs to a cruel little girl named Elizabeth Hubbard. She is one of the few that tried to have me condemned as a witch. As soon as I was released, I pulled it out of her chest."

"Note to self, don't challenge Tituba." I squeaked out. She laughed in delight.

"Now as far as your mother, I am not sure. I was not near her when she died. I heard about your birth and how the Shepherds came into the night and took you and your sister away from all of this."

I spat my tea all over the table while coughing. "Did you just say Shepherds?"

She got up, cleaning my face and the table like a grandma. "Yes, Marcy, Arthur and his wife Phillis Shepherd saved you and your sister."

"How?" I asked now trying to get the tea spots off my shirt.

"Well," she said sitting back down and letting out a sight trying to remember the past. "Arthur was a doctor and he is the one who delivered you in the jail and his wife Phillis was a bible study teacher in town. They were both very religious and loved everyone. Phillis was told by Arthur how strong of a fighter you were at birth given the conditions of the cell. So they decided that you and your sister couldn't die like that. The Shepherds told the town's judges that you had passed away from conditions to the cell and they encouraged them to let your sister go with them to be put in a mental institute."

"Are the Shepherds witches and just claim to be religious?"

Tituba looked at me for a moment then said, "No, I'm afraid they both have passed away a very long time ago. They had plenty of children and died of old age."

I kept my thoughts to myself as I continued on with my questions. "Last night, I fell through a door, is that a power of mine or is it because of this town?"

She shrugged, then asked, "Have you fallen through objects before?"

"No, but I did ask the door to open for me because I left the door key inside of the hotel room."

Tituba stood up and stretched, "You should coax more objects to see if it is a power you hold. I know you are curious and your devil of an aunt would never teach you."

My mind instantly went to my dream from last night. "Tituba, I had a dream last night that I…"

She cut me off mid-sentence by replying, "I know, child, I was there."

"My aunt was there too," I said to the palm of her hand.

"She will not rule your dreams anymore." I looked around her hand.

"So, is she like you and can go into others' dreams?"

Tituba lowered her hand. "Yes, but I do not use it for cruel reasons like she does, nor do I use reading minds for evil purposes."

I sat down like I had just been punched in the gut. That hypocritical bitch, I thought to myself. With a smile Tituba reading my mind said, "Yes, I agree with that analogy of your aunt."

I stood up feeling crunched for time. "Tituba, I have one last question, please?" She looked at me helping me put my coat on. "I think I'm having visions when I get touched but it's only when one person is touching me. He is a priest and in my visions or dreams or whatever the hell it is; he dies, or if I try to help him, then I die."

"What is your question, my dear?" I stood there for a moment, wishing I knew what my question was. "Is it a power of mine? Is it my aunt screwing with me to stay away from a man I like? Or am I crazy?" she hugged me and walked me to her door.

"I wish I knew what to tell you, Mercy Good, because it sounds like an awful thing." She went on while giving me a small box. "What I can tell you is that I took care of one theory you have," indicating my aunt ruining my dreams. "I also do not believe you are crazy." She smiled as I tried to hand her the box back afraid it was someone else's heart or worse. "Take it." She said reading the terror on my face and laughing, "I made it for you because I knew you were coming." With that, I got in my car and left.

Chapter Ten

I made it about halfway home when the snow began to fall. I drove through it as quickly and safely as possible to make it back in one piece. My thoughts were everywhere now that they were just mine to read and not Tituba. I thought what kind of objects I could coax or talk to. Could I get my dresser to move and dance for me like on Beauty and the Beast? That would be one hell of a party trick, I laughed to myself. As I entered Queens, the snow was moving fast and packed up pretty high. I was beginning to worry if my shop was okay or not. I know the flowers would be fine in the cold but not my Ira. Fat can only do so much for her and she would need a washcloth to make a nest with. Deciding my rodent needed me, I headed in that direction.

My store had power and heat, thank goodness. I made sure Ira had a washcloth that I cut up to help her make a nest with, and filled up her food and water. Knowing she would be fine now, I put my winter gloves back on as I made my way to the French doors, where I saw Father Ben standing with his fist raised like he was about to knock. I sighed, wishing this was not how my evening was going to start. Opening the door, he stood there shaking asking me "Goooood eeeevennnnning, Mmmmmarrrcccccyyy." I rolled my eyes at his politeness.

"Oh, for crying out loud!" I said as I pulled him in my shop. I shut the door and he began to rub his hands together.

"Thank you." He said as I shut the door.

"So," I said in an awkward tone watching him shiver. "Did you come here because you needed something or were you trying out for the 5k freeze dash?" He looked at me for a moment then chuckled. His smile was so handsome that it caused me to warm up a few degrees and I wasn't even cold!

He took a step towards me then thought for a moment and retracted it. Looking into my eyes he said, "Marcy, I am coming here as Father Benjamin. The Church and your city have come here to ask for your help." I looked up at him questioningly. He didn't stop himself this time as he took a deep breath in and stepped forward to me. He grabbed my little gloved hands in his, causing me to jump as though one of my terrible visions or dreams would happen. I waited for a moment and nothing happened. I let out a sigh of relief thinking it's gone. My aunt can't get me anymore. I finally could enjoy looking at his handsome face and get lost in those amazing eyes.

"Marcy?" He brought me back by saying my name in a concerned tone.

I looked up at him. "I'm sorry, what were you saying?"

He smiled and asked again not seeming upset that he had to repeat himself. "What I was saying is that this is the worst blizzard New York has had in years."

I looked at him a little confused. "Okay?" I asked waiting for him to finish telling me where he was going with this.

"Well, the trouble is there is a lot of homeless people in our city and most of them are war veterans." I squinted my eyes up at him and he began to hurry through his story knowing that I was starting to smell what he was stepping in. "My church can only hold so many of them and it's at maximum capacity, so I was wondering, since your shop is large in size, if we could also use it to get them out of the weather?"

I took a deep breath in to give myself a moment to get my emotions in check before replying, "Are you crazy?" I asked in a high tone that was almost a shout and dropping my hands from his. I guess breathing deep and checking my emotions didn't work very well, I thought as I went on yelling at him. "I don't have enough room in here for people." I had to come up with better reasons to validate my rejection. "What am I going to do with all of my flowers?" He stood there looking at me like I was just a cute little angry kitten that hissed at him. It was almost as if he was laughing at me on the inside.

He said in a very pleasant voice. "I can help you move as much as we can fit into your cooler." He said this with such kindness in his eyes and as his smile grew, he gathered up my hands again in his attempt to soften my rage. It worked a little. "Everything else we can put in the back room with your couch." I sighed, still not sure this was a good idea but then he added, "I will replace anything that gets damaged and it will just be until the blizzard lets up."

I looked down at the floor worried he was going to win this match by having a better hand on the river card, which if you played Texas Hold 'em, you'll know exactly what I'm talking about. Using his fingers, he gently brushed back my hair from my shoulder causing me to look up at him and stare into his eyes. His mouth was inches from mine as he said in a low voice. "Please, Marcy, they really need your help and not just them." His mouth moved mere inches away from my mouth and trailed along my cheek to my ear as he whispered, "I really need your help too." Damn it, I thought as I inhaled sharply at the feeling of his breath on my neck. He called my bluff and with the Ace of hearts coming out on the river he won me over with a royal flush.

"Fine," I sighed in defeat.

"Thank you, Marcy." He said with a smile and if I didn't know any better by the look in his eyes, he knew he won too. I felt a chill up my spine while looking at those victorious eyes that were now staring down at me. Did he play the same hand during the AA meeting? You asshole, I thought to myself.

"You know, I really don't like you sometimes." I said, causing us both to laugh as we began to carry my plants to the cooler.

Chapter Eleven

With my shop's floors cleared as much as possible, we began to bring in cots from the church's van that Ben had asked the Elders to bring us. As they were sent out to get the second load of cots Ben was greeting the homeless while I got all the blankets and pillows placed carefully on each cot. Everything seemed to be going well and I was actually starting to lighten up and feel like this was a good thing to do when Ben's phone rang. I watched him as he walked towards the front doors to hear well.

A moment later he came back to me and said, "With the weather, the Elders are not able to make it back to us with the rest of the cots."

I looked at him worried. Then looking outside, I said, "I'm assuming that means we can't get out either." He nodded standing next to me. "How many do we need?" I asked as he looked around scanning the room. It must be nice to be tall I thought looking up at him as he walked away. I would have to put a stepping stool on top of my desk to do the same thing.

After a couple of minutes, he returned and said, "I have two young men that don't have cots but they said they can make the floor work if we have extra blankets and also…" He got quiet. This had caused me to look up at him wondering why he stopped talking mid-sentence. "And also, what?" I asked encouraging him to continue. He looked down at me and finally said, "We don't have cots to sleep on."

I stood there for a moment thinking this couldn't be happening. "I'm sorry, what?" I asked in disbelief.

He could read the horror of my face and said as to reassure me. "It's fine, Marcy, you can lay on your couch and I can just try to get comfortable in a chair or something."

"What about your church?" I asked since little did he know that my face was not because of him but because of me.

"The Deacon is there to oversee the church." Oh no, I thought trying to remain calm. This was a bad idea because every time we were in the same place, I couldn't stop thinking of kissing him and wrapping more than my arms around him. He was like my favorite drink as an addict and I would know (as a loyal fake alcoholic, two months sober.)

He went to walk away from me and I grabbed his arm. "Father Ben, wait." He stopped and turned around to look at me. "We can share the couch. There is plenty of room." He smiled a very kind smile that made my heart stop in place.

Patting my arm, he said politely, almost afraid to bring up the past for fear that it might upset me. "When you were sick, we didn't fit on the couch very well."

I looked at him, a smile tugging at the corners of my mouth. "It has a pull out bed, fool."

He looked at me like he forgot to breathe for a moment and I think he did because he let out a deep breath and began to chuckle. "Oh." I gathered the pillows and blankets that were leftover and we walked to the back room together. He helped me pull the cushions from the couch. He suddenly stopped and while smiling from ear to ear, asked, "Did you just call me fool?"

I laughed on the inside and replied in a playful tone. "Yeah, but at least I said it to your face." I was joking on the outside but on the inside, I was terrified. What if I have dreams and he thinks I'm possessed. I've never been hit with holy water before. Will it burn or give me a bad breakout?

"Are you alright, Marcy?"

I looked up as he said my name, he was halfway under the covers of the pull out couch looking at me. I, on the other hand, was just standing there staring at my spot with my arms wrapped around myself. "Oh yes, I'm sorry. I'm just worried if everyone has plenty of stuff to keep warm."

His worry turned into happiness as he said, "They will be fine and you did a great thing today." Then he turned the blanket down on my side in an inviting manner. I looked from the spot meant for me up to him and my mind went in a completely different direction that it shouldn't have. Oh crap, what if we touch in our sleep!? I'm no wolf but he smelled so damn good and his body looked even better laying there on my couch like my prey. Was I strong enough to sleep next to this man and nothing more? What if I had a serious sleep condition that I didn't know about? With my flippin' luck, I can sleepwalk, sleep kiss or worse sleep hump! Is sleep humping a thing? I wondered to myself when I saw movement. It drew my attention back to him.

"It's alright, Marcy. Come lay down." He said it gently like he was trying to talk me down from jumping off a building. Boy, that was a good way of looking at it because in that moment as he stretched his hand out to me that's exactly how I felt. I got under the covers and laid there next to him. I felt tired and I don't know if it was the smell of him or the feel of his body next to mine giving me more than enough heat, I could feel sleep coming over me but I wasn't quite there yet. I heard him snore while thinking to myself, it must be nice to fall asleep that quick. Knowing I was only moments behind him to dreamland I took those moments to look into his handsome face studying his scars behind his ear. I wonder if that happened as a child or from war. I then looked down to where his hand was still stretched out wanting mine. I looked from my hand to his and couldn't believe how much bigger he was than me. They say curiosity killed the cat and as I finally gave in and laid my hand in his feeling his fingers begin to wrap around mine, I loved the feeling and how our hands seemed to fit with such difference. I began to lose vision and not because of sleep.

"Oh no," I mumbled out loud realizing that my dumbass was the cat.

Chapter Twelve

I felt the rain falling on my skin. "No," I begged out loud. My eyes closed tight hoping that this was anything, anything else than what I knew it to be. I heard the muffled voices talking in the church courtyard. I fell to my knees, "Please, no." I begged again opening my eyes to see the raindrops falling from strands of my hair in front of my face. I looked up to the sky as the lightning and thunder made their presence known. I felt warm water down my face realizing that it wasn't rain but my tears. "I don't know what to do please don't make me go through this again." I buried my face in my hands.

"Marcy?" I heard him calling my name but I couldn't move. "Marcy, wake up. Marcy!"

I awoke to him inches from me. His hands held my face as his thumbs were stroking my hair. His eyes were searching mine, desperately looking for an answer to my dreams. "What's wrong, Marcy, are you alright?" I couldn't hold myself together anymore as I began to sob. "Oh darling, don't cry." He had so much kindness in his voice as he wrapped his arms around me, pulling me into his arms. That only made me cry harder.

"I, I'm so sorry," I said around my sobs. I could feel his hands rubbing my back as he rocked me back and forth. "You have no reason to be sorry," he said listening to me sniffle as I sat up.

"I woke you." I answered as he handed me a tissue.

He chuckled, "No, I woke myself." I looked at him confused. As he read the confusion in my face he said, "Come with me." I followed him to the front of the store to where all of the homeless were sleeping. It was such a sad sight as I stood there hearing the groans of pain from some as they fought in their dreams. Some were even shouting and fighting in their sleep.

"Why are they doing that, are they in pain?" I asked looking grimly up at Ben. He went behind me and put his hands on my shoulders to make sure I could see everything as he spoke.

"Once you have seen and done what we all have, it never leaves you." As he went on, I could hear his voice begin to harden. "Post-Traumatic Stress Disorder or PTSD is a terrible thing. It haunts us not only in our dreams but in our lives as well. We lose our jobs, our families, and our homes because of it." As Ben continued, I could feel tears falling from my face as I stared at the guys I had just spent a few hours getting to know and the ones I did get to meet were great guys. "There is very little help out there for us so we turn to drugs, alcohol, and even violence. This is the end result for most of us," he said as he indicated to the group of sleeping men. "It can be very hard for us to function in day to day life with this problem."

I turned around to look at him for the first time and realized at this time he was the one fighting back tears as he stared back at his own kind, his fellow fighters, his brothers. I could tell in his face that his mind at this moment was fighting his own demons of both pain and anger for remembering what the world gave to those who fought for them. I couldn't begin to understand his past and everything that had happened, not only during but after, to them for only doing what they had to do for the sake of freedom. I gave him a hug wishing it could take away his pain and anguish. I felt him stiffen for a moment then as his body softened, he wrapped arms around me in return. I hugged him tighter not caring anymore. As we stood there, I realized for the first time that I needed him and he, right now, needed me back.

We spent the rest of the night wrapped up in each other's arms on the pull-out couch, talking. I asked him to tell me as many war stories as he would be willing to share with me, including the scar behind his ear. "It's a shrapnel wound." I was about to run my fingers across it to feel it but then I remembered that touching him caused me to fall into the vision of his death. Seeing that he was beginning to look tired I rolled over and said good night. "Good night, Marcy, and thank you for listening to me. It really helped me." He rolled away from me and after a few moments, I could hear him snoring. Finally, I was alone with my thoughts and began to wonder how it was that sometimes we can touch and nothing happens, while other times it's my worst nightmare.

Was it because of how I felt at the time? Maybe it was because I was standing in a certain spot like a random land Bermuda Triangle. Then it hit me like a jealous wife. I put my hand under my shirt touching his scar through the cloth. Nothing happened. I then took my hand out from beneath the blanket and touched his shirt. Again, nothing. It was all coming together now. Every time we touched and I didn't have my vision was because of clothes. Even when he held my hands before we got snowed in, he was wearing gloves. I was excited that I may have just cracked part of the case! However, I had to confirm it still and in order to do that, I would need to touch him, my skin to his. I didn't want to do this but I had to know so I could prevent it. Scared because I knew what was in store for me, I took my finger and as I began to shake from fear, I gently touched his shrapnel wound again.

Chapter Thirteen

I had my eyes closed as it started. I could feel that I was standing in water. It didn't seem to be deep water; it maybe went up to my ankles. This didn't feel the same as I realized I was not where I thought I would be. Opening my eyes for the first time I took in my surroundings. It was very hot and sunny with the desert winds howling around me. I stood in what looked to be some type of barley field. There was so much water where I was standing, I wondered how the plants didn't drown.

As I looked around and behind me, I saw what seemed to be a small town. I was about to head in that direction when the sound of tires crunching on the gravel road caused me to stop in my tracks. Uniformed men were approaching the town. There seemed to be two groups of five men walking right next to each other with a tan Humvee truck following closely behind the groups. I stood there watching them wondering where on earth I was and if they were friendly or not. I knew it had something to do with Ben but he isn't serving anymore, that I was aware of. Why was I brought here? What does this have to do with Ben?

Just as I thought his name, a soldier caught my eyes as he stood out from the rest and by that I mean he stood taller than the rest. He was second in the line and like everyone else he was carrying an automatic rifle, however, unlike the rest, he had a very large backpack on his back. He and the rest of his men were scouring the area as they walked ahead. I was a good distance from them but when I went to look at Ben's face, I saw that his eyes were already locked on me. He had spotted me before the rest of his group. I smiled at him and I believe he was about to smile back when an explosion happened just two guys behind him.

It all seemed to happen in a slow-motion replay. The explosion happened, causing the fourth guy in line to vanish. The fifth guy flew back and his head hit on the front of the truck. The Third guy was thrown into Ben who fell along with the first man in line. I covered my ears unable to hear anything but a high pitched noise. As my hearing started to come back, I could hear men shouting from within the group as some of the men got up and others didn't. I could hear one man shouting over everyone else. He must be in charge of the mission they were on. "Shepherd is wounded, someone get a first aid kit to treat him so he can get up and help the others, then have him call in a medevac," he yelled.

I felt my heart drop as I heard he was hurt. I saw red near his face. Why was this being shown to me? Am I his angel of death? I wondered as it seemed there was never a happy ending for him in my visions. I watched helplessly from afar as I saw two men covering him then he was beginning to stand up with their help. He was going to be okay, I thought happily as I wanted to run over and throw my arms around him. He was up and with blood still coming from what looked like his neck, began to check on the other two men that were down. While rummaging through his large medical backpack, he got on his radio and gave their location for a medevac to come and take his injured men. We were in Afghanistan of all places.

The helicopter finally arrived after what seemed like a lifetime, and as the injured men were loaded onto the medevac, I thought surely he would get on too since he was hurt. But no, he waved his arms to let the pilot know he was good to continue. He picked up his backpack and gun from where he was treating his men and they resumed their walk to the town, as though nothing had happened. But just as they reached the beginning of the town, Ben looked in my direction again and I saw sadness in his eyes. Then he was gone and so was I.

Chapter Fourteen

A few days had gone by with us still stuck in my shop together. During that time, I saw a completely different side of Ben. He was back with people who understood his monsters as he understood theirs. I even think I heard him curse once! We were having dinner and I asked him when he wasn't chatting with one of the guys, "How often do you get sent overseas?"

He looked to me and said, "I am not in the military anymore."

"Oh," I said as I placed some green beans in my mouth to chew that over before asking about what I saw.

He smiled and grabbed my hand as he said. "I wish you would let me look at your hands," examining the wraps I used to protect myself from seeing things I didn't want to see.

I pulled my hand out of his and went on, "Why are you not serving anymore?"

He looked at the spot in his empty hand like he was disappointed I didn't keep mine there longer. "I got injured in Afghanistan."

I stared at him hoping he would continue. Thankfully, he did, as he saw I was still looking at him. "I was doing a standard patrol with two squads of five guys each. We approached a village and we were wanting to go around it but couldn't because there was a dike on both sides of the road for irrigation." He stopped talking for a moment and took a breath in. "This caused us no choice but to take the road through and at about a half a mile before the village entrance our first guy, myself, and the guy behind me managed to miss a land mine. Our fourth guy Nickilson wasn't so lucky."

"Ben," I said, to stop him before he went any further. I was angry at myself for letting him get this far into the story knowing it might trigger something in him that he didn't want to relive.

He knew what I was trying to do and replied, "It's okay, I'm fine." Then he resumed his story, "It killed him instantly. The impact from the bomb caused the guy behind me to be thrown into me and me into the guy that was first in line. I had shrapnel go through my neck." I felt like I was there again listening to him, then I looked around realizing that I wasn't the only one listening as the rest of our table was quiet listening to Ben's every word. "After that, we continued on. Once it was over, I was sent home." We continued eating dinner.

The guys were all still talking and laughing together once the meal was over. I, on the other hand, was sitting on the pull out couch, lost in my own mind. I felt like I took one step forward in making a breakthrough with knowing that touching his skin with mine would cause my visions only to then take two steps back with this curveball. Why did it show me his past this time instead of his future? I pulled my knees up to my chest feeling the weight of the world on my head. "May I come in?" It was Ben leaning on the door frame. He looked so handsome standing there that I could just stare at him all day.

"Of course," I replied. "This is technically your room too until the storm lets up, then you're out on your ass." I shot him a wink causing him to chuckle.

He climbed on the pull-out next to me and grabbed my pillow out from under me, causing my head to fall to the mattress with a thud. "Hey, that's mine," I exclaimed trying to get it back from him. He and I laughed together and he finally gave me back the pillow by throwing it over my face. "I enjoy this Ben much better over Father Ben," I said with a big smile on my face as I elbowed him in the side. He quit laughing and with a mischief look on his face pulled me in for a hug.

"This Ben is broken." He said around a yawn then out of nowhere he kissed my shoulder almost at my neck. I froze for a moment waiting for him to apologized or see the regret in his face for doing it. Neither of those happened. Smiling on the inside I snuggled myself close to him inhaling his old spice smell and kissing his chest.

"Broken isn't always a bad thing," I mumbled and drifted off to sleep listening to him snore.

The next morning was nice because the snow was manageable now that the plows could get the removal taken care of. We went out to let the guys know the good news and it was mixed emotions for sure from everyone. We were all happy to not be stuck anymore and at the same time, we all grew close. I let them all know that they would always have somewhere here as long as they don't break my shit or hurt my rat. We all laughed at poor Ira for a moment. The church van came to collect the cots and everyone helped. Ben said tonight if everyone wanted to come to the church, he would make a soup dinner. Everyone was now gone leaving me with Ben. I began to go through my inventory to move the flowers back onto the show floor. He started to help. Once everything was put back in place flower wise, we went to the backroom to put the couch back together.

"Gotta say, I'm gonna miss fun Ben." I teased and was met with a pillow to the face for it.

"I'm always fun Ben," he said. As to prove his point he playfully pushed me onto the fold-out. I got back up and for some dumb reason, I thought I was tough enough to return the favor. As I attempted to push him so he would fall as I did, he grabbed my arms and pulled me down with him. I was lying on top of him now with his hands still holding my arms tight. I was laughing and trying to wiggle off of him at the same time with no such luck.

"Ben, I'm probably squishing you with my fatness, let me up."

I kept wiggling as he laughed and replied, "You're not fat and you're not hurting me either, though you really need to stop moving around so much because God can only help me so much as a man." I instantly flinched in pain and began to feel my face going red as I felt what I was unintentionally doing to him.

I was too scared to look at his face so I turned my head instead, letting my hair cover my face from him as I asked. "Ben, can you let me up." He moved my hair to the side exposing how red my face was.

"What do you say?" he asked in a half teasing/ half priest voice. A smirk pulled on my lips as I looked into his face now letting my eyes search his.

I wanted him to think I was all into the moment as I whispered, "Bite me."

He groaned and rolled us both on the bed to where he was on top pinning me under him his hand holding my arms over my head. I felt him press the weight of his hips into me as I moved around for a moment then he buried his face in my hair taking in my scent as he groaned in my ear, "You don't play fair."

Finally, after a moment, he released me letting me up from his grip. I laughed and said, "That's not the pot calling the kettle black."

He thought for a moment and while grinning said, "Fair enough." Looking around, I saw everything was back in order so I looked at Ben who was watching me. Realizing that I was looking at him now he said, "Well, I suppose I should go back to the church to see how everything managed and to start with the soup dinner." I could tell he was a little disappointed leaving me but I had so much to do and I know he did too.

"Whatever blows your pantyhose, pal."

He thought that one for a minute and asked, "Do you have your own language or something?"

I answered by throwing his coat at him and saying, "It's been fun, bye Felecia!" He walked past me putting his coat on and laughing so hard I could still hear him after the front door was shut.

Chapter Fifteen

I finally made it home where I grabbed a bowl of cereal. After eating, I decided a long hot bubble bath would help me think. I got my phone and a towel placing them on the side stand next to my tub and picked Shinedown to play as I ran the water. As I sat watching the bubbles rise, I began to think what my next move would be. I needed more help to understand my powers and visions. The only witch I knew that had any type of knowledge of powers was Tituba. I turned the water off and lowered myself down into the tub letting the hot water burn my skin. It felt amazing to let the water swallow me as I laid there. I had missed my bathtub so much since I swear I am part hippo.

Surprisingly, the bath wasn't helping as much as it usually did with my thoughts everywhere. I laid there wondering if I should go try to see Tituba again. Would she know of any other witches around my area that can teach me magic? Should I check the personals on Craigslist? How would I even post something on Craigslist? Maybe I could write something like, "Teach me magic." Hey, I've read way worse on Craigslist personals like, "Would you just look at it?" I laughed remembering that poor guy that was on there for months and months wanting a woman to just look at it.

Getting myself back on track I figured maybe I could just try with my kitchen table or my bedroom door first before paying Tituba another visit. Deciding that was my best option I drained the water from the tub and wrapped my very soft robe around me. Going out into my bedroom I glanced in the direction of my kitchen area. Putting my hands on my hips I said loud and proud to myself, "I know what I need to do!" as I headed in the direction of my bed and slid under the covers. I know, I know but a nap sounded so much better than effort. It's one of those hashtag-sorry-not-sorry moments. As I began to fall asleep feeling clean and warm, I began to think of Ben. I really needed to start keeping more distance from him because it was getting harder and harder to keep him out of my mind and as he had me pinned under him at the shop, I could tell it was getting hard for him too. I groaned out thinking how amazing he felt on top of me. I felt like he wanted to cause me pain as he had my arms gripped so tight above my head in his hands. It felt amazing to me that I wanted it to hurt more. I smashed any other thoughts of what I wanted before I became too excited to sleep.

I checked my phone for the time and it was only 2 pm so I figured around 5 pm I would start my magic. The next thing I know, I'm waking up and its 8 am the next day. Woops, I thought getting up. So much for doing the magic at home I thought while cursing myself for the nap. I got dressed and barely made it to work on time. Again, not that it mattered but as I got my keys out of my pocket to unlock the door, I found a wrapped package laying on the doorstep. I picked it up thinking it was too early for any deliveries and a note fell from the box. "Marcy, I hope you have a wonderful day." It was signed, "Ben." I opened the box to see a beautiful wooden carved rose. I brought it in, placing it on my desk. Seeing the rose now presentable on my desk, I began to work on my orders. I had quite a few more than usual but I got them taken care of in no time.

2 pm came quickly and with everything in the shop settled down I decided to close early and work on my witch tasks. I moved the Gerbera Daisies from my middle showroom table, clearing it off. I thought of myself going through the table while leaning my weight against it. Nothing was happening as I stood that way for what seemed like an eternity. I began to feel like a fool, thankful that no one could see what I was doing since I had the blinds closed. I finally stood up and wondered if it was because the table was metal instead of wood. I was about to try leaning through my desk when the bell to my shop went off. Feeling like a teenager who just got caught smoking I yelled out, "I wasn't doing anything!" and I stood up in a hurry.

A man came in with holes through his shoes and his clothes. He was about my height and thin like a bendy straw. His hair was in all directions like a crazy man but it didn't look bad on him nor did the scruff on his face. I looked a little surprised wondering what he needed at my store.

"What can I help you with?" I asked starting to think by the smile on his face that he might be here to rob me.

"Marcy, right?" he asked as he took a step in my direction.

I nodded taking a half a step back. "Did you want to order any flowers?" I asked as I started to get more and more nervous.

"No, hun' it's me, Matt." I stared at him blankly as he went on realizing that his name didn't trigger anything. "I stayed here during the blizzard storm."

"Oh, hey!" I said now realizing that made more sense than him coming in for flowers. I did promise all of them that they are welcome here. "You glad the snow is all melted?" I asked starting to relax now that I somewhat knew the guy.

"I'm happy, but now it's supposed to rain a lot in the next few weeks."

I frowned, "That stinks, do you go stay in a shelter when it rains?"

He shrugged and replied, "I stay where ever I can."

I felt bad after hearing that. I was much luckier than others. "Well, you can hang out here for the day if you have nothing better going on," I replied sitting at my desk to do some online orders that just came in. I began wondering why I have been getting a lot of orders since the blizzard when I got an alert on my computer.

"Thank you, ma'am."

He sat in one of the chairs near the door and watched me as I continued staring at the computer. "Local pastor falls three stories from the church's bell tower and dies." I must have had quite the look on my face because Matt asked me if I was okay. I looked up at him wondering if talking to him would be a mistake or not, so I tested the waters by replying. "Oh, I'm fine just reading about the pastor that died today."

He nodded as he asked, "Is that the one who fell from the top of the church?" I didn't feel anything out of the ordinary from him and it was nice to talk to someone besides my rat, so, for the remainder of the day, we chatted as I worked.

Once the day was over, I locked the door and it was a clear night out, so after I said good night to Matt, I began to walk home instead of taking the bus. I had started getting a weird feeling as I got about halfway home like I was being followed.

I would nonchalantly glance over my shoulder but I wouldn't see anyone. So I assumed I was crazy and kept trucking. When I got to the alley at 3rd and Harris, I was flown into the wall, my cheek hitting the brick so hard I thought my teeth were going to break. I tried to scream for help but whoever had me pinned was already two steps ahead of that as a cloth was placed over my nose and mouth. I was moving as much as I could while still trying to scream around the cloth covering my face. I felt hands in my pockets and tugging on my purse strap. As the strap on my shoulder snapped off, I got a glance at my attacker.

It was Matt, the same Matt who lived in my shop for days during severe weather and the same Matt whom I had in my store just today. Out of nowhere, I felt myself flying back onto the ground but it wasn't because of who was holding me to the wall but because someone else was throwing Matt off of me and I ended up going along for the ride. I sat up about to run when I saw the hand of the one saving me.

Chapter Sixteen

"Marcy, Marcy get up, honey, we need to leave!" I sat on the ground looking up at Ben who was continuously looking between me and where Matt was laying. He had his hand stretched out to help get me up off the ground. I was struggling to move though, as my mouth began to taste like pennies and my head hurt like a mother trucker. I was still sitting on the ground like a dumbass looking at Ben's outstretched hand when I saw movement behind him. Matt was trying to get up from where Ben left him in a pile on the ground. I attempted to warn him that Matt was getting up. However, my voice wasn't coming out. I ended up mouthing Matt and pointing behind Ben. He looked at where Matt was almost back up to standing and instantly left me to go make sure he didn't make the mistake of getting up again.

I would tell you play by play of how Ben fought Matt but honestly, it wasn't as cool as what you read in a comic book where there is "BAM" and "POW" that you can see inside of speech balloons. Between the noises, blood and the sound of bones breaking it was actually quite gruesome to watch. I would have gotten sick had I not seen worse from my visions or whatever they were. "Do not ever come near Marcy again, do you hear me!?" he yelled it at Matt who laid there next to the dumpster that he got knocked into for the final blow. "If you are seen within one hundred feet of her, I will make sure you don't live to see the sunrise." With that, he walked back to me and knowing by this time that I was too injured, too scared, or too dumb to get myself up he picked me up himself. Setting me on my feet he asked if I could walk. I nodded that I could so he grabbed my hand and walked me out of the alley. We turned in the direction of my store instead of the direction of my home.

Once at my shop, he looked at me for my purse so he could get the keys to the door then closed his eyes looking angry realizing that it was still in the alley with an unconscious Matt. He looked at me saying, "Sorry for this,

I'll replace it."

"Replace wha…?" was as far as I got before Ben kicked my beautiful French doors in causing them to open. I was about to chew him out for that until he grabbed my hand again and pulled me into the back room. As soon as we were back there, he gave me a once over, he started with my head moving my hair around to look for any kind of cuts. Then he looked at my face.

"Your cheek is cut pretty bad; we will need to put something on that."

"That must be why my mouth tasted like pennies," I replied as he went on examining me by pulling the sleeves of my shirt then lifting my shirt to check my stomach and sides for anything. I went to protest as my shirt went up pretty far as he was looking, but then he lowered my shirt enough that I could tell in his face that he didn't want to hear it. I had never met serious hard-ass military Ben, I thought. He was kind of scary. I watched not wanting to poke the bear by talking as he finished his once over.

Once he was satisfied that I was not badly injured he lowered my shirt back down allowing me to finally say something. "We should have called the police instead of you hurting him and threatening his life." I'm not sure if he didn't hear me, or he just didn't care as he grabbed my arms and shook me back and forth almost shouting in my face like a drill instructor. "What the Hell were you thinking, walking home alone with that guy?" I tried to tell him that I wasn't walking home with anyone. I was being followed but he kept yelling that I couldn't say anything. "Do you realize how many women get hurt every day for doing something so careless like you just did? Why didn't you take the bus home or call me to take you home? Answer me!" he roared in my face demanding I explain myself. Now I know most of you think I'm a boss who wakes up every morning all hot shit but to be honest, I'm kind of a pansy when I get yelled at so my only reply was crying. Seeing that he made me cry, I'm pretty sure it made him more upset but then, instead of yelling at me more or breaking the rest of my shop, he just pulled me into a tight hug burying his face into my hair. I was beyond confused as to what was happening so I just stood there like a flamingo. After a few moments of this, he let me out of his embrace and locked his eyes with mine. "Don't you realize, I wouldn't know what to do if something bad had happened to you?" he said as he brushed my hair from my face. "Don't do that to me again, please." He begged, pulling me to him as he kissed me.

His kiss was the kind of kiss that has no words to describe it. It touched me from head to toe and everywhere in between.

I could feel my legs and hands shaking as I felt like I was going to fall I wrapped my arms around his neck and let out a small moan. Hearing my delight, I felt Ben pick me up as he carried me to the couch. Oh, that poor couch must hate me by now, I thought as he laid me down on it. I felt like I wasn't breathing and the way he was kissing me, I didn't even care. What a way to go, I thought as I felt his hands move from my face to my sides. I was fading and I could feel myself leaving again. Crap, I was just joking, I thought as I felt the light from my vision dimming. It was over like in theatre as the curtain closed on me. Exit stage, left.

Chapter Seventeen

I was standing in the church this time. This is strange to be in a new place, I thought but I heard the rain and lightning so it must be my vision from before. I went to run outside, when I heard voices from the hallway in church causing me to stop. The voices were coming near me so out of panic I ducked down under a pew, careful not to be seen. I looked at a pamphlet that was tucked in one of the bibles, it had a date of a month from now. I felt like this was a good thing to give me a rough guess on when I had to know and learn my powers to save or prevent Ben from dying, or myself, for that matter.

The voices sat up at the front of the church and began to talk about Ben. "The church hasn't been the same since Father Shepherd." Oh no, I thought. This is to show me life after he is gone like on A Christmas Carol. I curled myself into a ball trying hard to keep my tears from falling as I felt my heartbreaking. I listened carefully as the men went on. "He was so caring for everyone and we had the most attendance ever in the church's history when he was with us."

Unable to hear any more, I began to quietly make my way to the door on the side which led me to the courtyard. The stone table was there and I wanted nothing more but to die in that moment. I laid my hand on the table and cried out his name. I wondered how I could feel this strongly about him. As the rain poured on me all I could think was how I didn't want to live a life he was not in. It hit me at once, causing me to feel so empty and cry harder. I felt this way because I was in love with him but he was gone.

I woke to a flashlight in my eye. I backed my face away quickly only to feel a hand holding me still. "Careful sweetheart, I think you have a concussion from when you fell."

I sighed at Ben who was still flashing a tiny flashlight in my eyes. "I'm fine, Ben," I said swatting the light from my face. I sat up staring at him wishing I could tell him everything but Pixie advised I do no such thing.

"Almost every time we touch, you blackout though, you must be allergic to me or something." This must have been his attempt to joke but his face looked too concerned about me that I just looked at him.

"It's not that," I said desperately trying to fish for an excuse. "I just have a very severe case of germophobia, that's all."

He bowed his head as he said so quietly, "Oh gosh, I am so sorry, Marcy. I never meant to cause you such distress over my selfish wanting for you."

I was about to say it's fine but I realized what he said as my brain caught up. "You want me?" I asked feeling stunned.

His eyes softened looking into mine. "More than anything I have ever wanted before." He went to reach for my hands then stopped himself. I smiled as I pulled the sleeves to my sweater down to cover my hands, causing him to chuckle, and he held them for a moment then pulled me into an embrace.

"Is this okay?" he asked hesitantly. I hugged him back harder. "This feels great, don't let me go."

"I don't think I can." He said as he brushed my hair to the side and began to rub my back. "But I really need to go check in at the church to see if the guy that attacked you has made it there yet."

I pulled away from him to search his face. "Will you get into trouble for it?"

He shrugged, "I'm not sure, to be honest, but I would do it again if someone was trying to hurt you. May I see you tomorrow?" He asked as he put his coat on looking at me.

"I can make us dinner if you would like," I replied not hiding my smile very well.

Pulling me to him again he murmured, "That sounds wonderful."

Chapter Eighteen

It was surprisingly a nice day out as I left my house the next day. The temperature was warming up, allowing the ground to dry from the snow and rain. Feeling the warmth from the sun on my face, I decided I should just take the day and go work on my powers. No more screwing around, Marcy, I thought to myself, determined as I began walking in the direction of the Cunningham Park. It was a very large park with trails, small creeks, and wooded areas so that I shouldn't be noticed. As I arrived, I decided to try the trails as I walked for an area that looked to have little to no foot traffic.

I found the perfect spot. It had a small creek and many trees to hide myself from others. I should start small, I said to myself, finding a smaller tree. I placed my hand on it and said to it in a powerful badass tone, "I am Marcy Good and you will bow before me!" The tree didn't move. Crap, I thought stepping back and attempted again with a spell that rhymed. "Now is the time and here is the place, for you, a tree, to bow to my grace." Still, the tree didn't budge. "What is your problem, damn it!?" I yelled at the tree and snapped one of its branches off hoping that would make me feel better but it didn't. I sighed as I knelt to the ground wondering if what had happened in Salem was just a hallucination I had.

As I stood up, I felt like my hand was stuck and as I looked, I realized in disbelief that the branch in my hand was caught on some vines but more importantly the branch was halfway through my hand! I about shrieked until I saw that I wasn't bleeding and it must have happened like the door trick in Salem. "I'm not crazy!" I yelled as I jumped up in joy which also caused me to whack myself in the face forgetting for a second that I still had a branch through my hand. "Oh crap, I have a branch through my hand." I began to panic as to how I was going to get it undone without hurting myself or others.

"Would you stop yelling before someone sees you?!" I looked up to the trail to see a dark-haired man who was thin and tall. He made his way down to where I was and grabbed my wrist.

"Don't," I began to say closing my eyes hard as our hands touched.

After a moment nothing happened so I opened my eyes and he was looking at me like I just grew moose antlers. I laughed nervously as I spoke. "I got this! Thank you for trying to help me."

He replied by raising an eyebrow, "Just how will you get this taken care of? I assume by your shouting you don't know how to get it out of your hand."

I still figured he was a human so I know they are all about the doctors. "I will just go to the ER and get it taken care of."

"You can't go to the ER!" they will ask questions and you'll bring them down on all of us.

I blinked at him and after a moment asked, "Are you a witch too?"

He looked offended but as I was about to backpedal, he said, "I am no witch, I am a warlock, there is a big difference."

He touched the branch in my hand and was quiet for a moment. I watched in amazement as the stick turned into ash. I felt relief and as I went to thank him, he dropped my hand and turned away to walk back up to where a woman and two children stood waiting for him. "Wait, please!" I ran after him up the hill still going on. "Can you teach me how you did that?"

He kept climbing not looking at me as he replied, "No."

This had caused me to stop for a moment then I replied up to him. "I don't know anyone else that can teach me what my powers are. Wait."

He stopped and turned around with a horrified look on his face. "Are you the idiot who put a post on Craigslist!?"

I looked at him blankly before answering, "I thought I wrote a very tasteful ad, thank you."

"Oh Archer, just hear her out." This came from his very petite wife with strawberry blond hair who made me feel tall for once. "If we don't help her then she could get us into trouble posting more ads."

He looked very unpleased at what she was saying. "Ellie, my love, I really don't think this is the best idea. I don't feel comfortable having a stranger around you and the children, to begin with, and this one is a witch with no control over her powers."

She thought that one over for a moment then replied, "Mia and Kaden have their spring break on Friday. Perhaps we could send them to Indiana to be with my family for the week." He looked up at her and she quickly added, "You can put that protective spell that you used on me that time you had the flu." He growled in defeat as she said with a smile, "Then it's settled. Give her our address then get up here so we can finish our walk."

He told me their address then looked down at me which wasn't hard since he was already 6'3" but he, at this time, was also further up the hill to make him look even taller. He pointed his finger in my face as he told me, "Know this, witch. If you make any harmful moves or spells towards my Ellie or our home, I will turn you into the ashes just like the branch that was stuck in your hand." With that, he walked the rest of the way up the hill to his wife reaching for her hand. They left with their children riding bikes in front of them.

"Well, that escalated quickly," I said to myself as I climbed up the hill to get a last look at my new teacher who had just threatened my life.

Chapter Nineteen

"I finally found someone who can teach me but I don't do well with mean people. They make me cry and what if I cry too much where he won't show me my powers, then I won't have a teacher. What am I gonna do?" I collapsed onto my favorite white chaise, spilling my heart out only to have Pixie tell me yet again that she was not a damn therapist. "If I pay for you to go back to school can ya make that work for me?" I asked with my face buried into the chaise. She giggled but did not accept my offer.

"What did you say this warlock's name was again?" she asked as she accepted a bird onto her arm.

I replied with a sigh, "Archer."

Her eyes were wide as she spun around so fast causing her crow to fall from her arm. "Oh Milos, my love, I am so sorry!" She picked the crow up and hugged him apologetically. He squawked at her then took off. She looked where he left for a moment before looking back at me. "I can't believe you are having him teach you, he is a very powerful warlock but he is so unkind. I crossed paths with him seventy or eighty years back and my poor crow, Remy, made the mistake of taking a watch of his and he turned Remy into a rat!" I looked at her wondering why that was a bad thing. She read my questioning face and said, "He wouldn't listen to me after that. I can only control the creatures of the sky." She raised her arm to let her second bird land. "Thank you, Horace," she said as the bird dropped a small jewelry box into her hand.

"I need help badly, Pix, I can't let Ben die without trying to do everything I can."

She sighed, then smiled as she pulled from the tiny jewelry box, a diamond ring. "Would you be doing all of this if it was anyone else in danger?"

I eyed her wondering where she was going with this. "Yes," I croaked.

"Lies! You are in love with the priest," she shrieked as she jumped up and clapped her hands together. I buried my face further into the chaise hoping if I left it there long enough it would kill me. As if reading my mind, she came over and pulled my shoulders up and said in my ear, "Did you guys kiss yet?" I sighed as I felt my face get hot while thinking of Ben's kiss and how much I wanted it again. "OMG lady, you so did!"

I rolled over onto my back, "Yeah, but every time we touch with our skins I get thrown into a vision of his and it kinda ruins the moment, ya know?" I looked up to her as she frowned.

"That would suck," she said looking at her front door, "I would probably shrivel up and die if I couldn't kiss Rune."

I glared at her, "Is this supposed to help me, Pixie? Because it's not." I sat up giving her more room next to me. "Anyway, I'm hoping that by learning from Archer, I can fix this and hopefully, I can kiss Ben without watching him die." I looked over to her as she stood up accepting a bird. "Also, not sure how this Archer guy was back then but his wife seems to soften his heart so that's a plus for me."

She held the bird for a moment longer than usual whispering something to it and kissing its forehead before letting it go. "Whatever helps you sleep at night, my dear," she said putting the item she was given in her purse.

I stood up and stretched getting ready to leave. "What did you say to him?"

She looked at me confused for a moment then realized I was talking about her bird. "Oh, Milos is angry with me so I was telling him that I was sorry and I will make it up to him with livers later." She ignored my gagging sound as she sent a text on her phone and went on. "He stole from one of my ex-boyfriends but I'm not sure if he did that on purpose because he was angry with me or not. So, needless to say, I will be expecting a visit soon." I asked her if she wanted me to stay in case the ex gets upset but she declined and said she already sent a text to Rune and he is on his way over. I gave her a hug and left to go by my shop to get ready for my dinner date with Ben.

I made lazy lasagna for dinner and waited for him to arrive. I wasn't the best dressed but I didn't smell and I really liked the shirt I had on, to be honest. It was pretty, black, and very lacy. I was so nervous he wouldn't show up but when he finally did, my anxiety went away. I opened the door to greet him. He took a moment to take in my look and said, "I am not good with expressing myself or emotions, but wow." I became nervous again, not knowing what he meant by that and he must have seen the distressed look on my face because he grabbed the sleeves to my shirt and said, "You look beautiful."

Chapter Twenty

Dinner with Ben, just him and I, was beyond wonderful. We had a chance to talk and get to know more about one another. Once I broke it to him that I was not an actual alcoholic, we surprisingly had a lot in common and liked the same things. We were laughing together as I said to him, "Wait, you are a priest and you like Rock music?"

He replied with a smirk, "Hey, we lived off of that kind of music when we were fighting overseas."

I looked at him knowing what I saw when he was there. "Thank you for your service."

He got quiet for a moment before replying, "Don't thank me; thank the guys who didn't get to come home. They made the ultimate sacrifice."

He stood up, "Thank you for dinner. Would you like help with the dishes?"

I looked at the table thinking he was crazy because the plates and cups were plastic. "Nah, I got them." A smile pulled at the corners of his mouth as he came to my side of the table. He stood so damn tall right next to where I sat, causing me to look up at him.

"I had a great night," he said as he held his hand out for me. Then remembering that I can't touch his skin, he said in a commanding tone. "Stand up." Chills went up to my spine with excitement as I stood up.

He moved my hair from my shoulders to expose my neck and collar bone as he asked. "I can only touch you where you have clothes on, correct?" I began to shake as I whispered yes. The next thing I know, he is picking me up by causing me to wrap my legs around him. My arms wrapped around his neck careful not to touch him with my hands. He pushed me against the wall still holding me tight. I gasped in surprise and delight as he began to move my arms above my head while grinding his hips against mine. We were both breathing hard and he stopped to look at my flushed face. "Marcy, may I kiss you?" every part of me wanted to say yes but I knew what would happen if I let him so I kissed a trail on his chest up to his shoulder smoothing out his shirt before I gently bit him. He roared out in pleasure and moved my hair to the side holding it with his hand exposing my neck to return the favor.

"Ben, please." I pleaded to him not to, but hell, at this point I didn't even believe myself. I wanted every part of this and damn it I wanted it now.

A powerful wind hit my already broken French doors with such power that it knocked one completely down, breaking the glass. This had caused us both to jump. Ben put me down and walked to the front room to pick the door up when a woman came into the store. She looked at me with hate in her eyes as she looked down at Ben. It was my aunt Abby. He stood up and said, "Can I help you, ma'am?"

"You can stay away from my niece." She pointed at me, "She has no business being with you even if it's just short term since you are a priest and she is a witch." Ben just stood there looking at her like she was crazy.

Then as he looked at her more, he said, "I know you from somewhere." Thinking about it a moment more it finally hit him and by his expression, you'd have thought he had seen a ghost. "You are the woman from my dreams."

Rage instantly went through me as he said that and I charged up to my aunt yelling, "You were in his dreams!?" I was almost to her when I felt arms wrap around my midsection. "How dare you!"

I began to claw at her but Ben held me back. "Marcy, stop!" But I couldn't stop seeing red as I wanted to hurt her as much as she hurt me, my sister, and now the man I love.

"She doesn't deserve to live, Ben, let me go!"

My aunt Abby had a wicked smile on her lips as she said to Ben, "Yes Ben, let her go." As she said it, she moved her hand and it caused his arms to release me. I fell to the floor with a thud, landing on my stomach. She walked over to me and grabbed me by my hair. I groaned in pain as I felt her ripping out strands of my hair. She pulled my face close so I was looking up at Ben who at the moment wasn't moving as though he was confused but most likely under a spell. "Don't worry, Marcy; I wasn't the only one in his dreams."

As she said the last part, Ben looked at me with sadness in his eyes. "I would like to leave, please," he said, still looking at me. I began to feel tears going down my cheeks.

"Ben, please don't go." My aunt released my hair to undo whatever she had done to Ben. He could move and as he began to walk towards me, I reached out for him and he moved out of my reach as he walked past.

I watched him leave, then turned to her still very angry, "Why did you do that?" I was met with her hand. She hit so hard it felt like I had gotten vertigo as I fell to the ground.

"You are the stupidest little girl that I have ever met," she said to me pulling me by my hair again as she went on. "A priest, of all people, Marcy! Surely you were not dropped on your head that much." She dropped me to the floor again letting that be her final words as she left. I sat up after a moment and sighed. I picked the door up and attempted to put it back on its hinges. It was going to be fine for the night.

I was too tired and numb to go home so I just grabbed a blanket from the back and made myself comfortable on the couch. My aunt was such a monster to do that but she was right. You should have seen how Ben was looking at me when she said we were witches who invaded his dreams. I could never be someone good for him. This didn't mean I still couldn't save him from my own kind. He may not love me anymore but he still didn't deserve to die. I wish I could rewind time to prevent what had just happened. Though, if I could rewind time then I would not have gone to that damn AA meeting, to begin with. I felt like I couldn't win either way because he also saw me the next morning at work.

Feeling defeated, I looked up at the lion faces on the wall tears beginning to fall. "I'm damned if I do and damned if I don't," I said rolling away from their stares to face the couch.

Chapter Twenty-One

I woke up the next morning early. I checked my phone and Ben had not called or texted me. I sent him a text apologizing for last night and that I hoped he had a good day today. I gave Ira food and water then made a call to have my doors fixed. Throwing my hair up in a bun and putting a sweatshirt with sweatpants on I headed to Archer and Ellie's house to begin my training. Their house was a Victorian-style home that was massive both on the outside and on the inside. I knocked on the door and after a brief moment Ellie answered with a huge smile as well as a rather tall and grumpy looking Archer standing directly behind her as she asked, "Ready to train?" I stood there for a moment taking in how she was such a kind and beautiful woman that it honestly blew my mind how she ended up with a dill weed like Archer.

"I'm ready!" I replied and she squeaked in delight turning around to let me in and bumped into her husband, not knowing he was standing there. As she stumbled back, he instantly was holding her steady while cupping her face in his hands apologizing to her. She laughed it off and said she was fine but he still made sure for himself before giving her a kiss on her forehead.

"Darling, could you go make us tea, please?" he said as he held her hand walking in the direction of the kitchen.

She made a huff and said in a disappointed tone, "Archer, you said I could watch and you even put the spell on me and the house so no one would get hurt." Her pouty face must have been his kryptonite because as soon as she stuck out her bottom lip, he gave in.

"Fine, damn it, but you have to sit where I tell you to. Do you hear me?"

As we walked to the library I asked him quietly, "Is Ellie not a witch?"

He looked at me and said, "No, she is a normal human, as are our children, as far as we know." I looked at him before asking but he must have already known where I was going with this. "I have an ageing curse I put on myself so I could age with her. She is my sunshine and I am her moon so it only makes sense that we either exist together in this world or we don't." We got to the library and he told Ellie that she would need to go sit at the top of the staircase and she obliged. He turned his attention to me, "Are you ready to begin?"

I looked from him up to Ellie, who all but had a foam finger out for me. I looked back at him and said with confidence, "I'm ready, where do we start?"

He looked away from me and grabbed a book from the shelf. Then he handed it to me and said, "Put your hand through this book."

I stared at the book for a moment, then at him. "How do I do it though, do I say a spell, do I wiggle my spirit fingers, or do I envision myself going through the book?"

As I asked this, he looked up at Ellie then at me stunned, "Wait, you don't know how to use your powers at all?"

I nodded my head. "I don't even know what powers I have, to be honest," I admitted quietly.

"Are you kidding me?" he asked almost shouting. "Where the hell have you been where you couldn't learn your powers?"

It took a good hour and a half of me explaining my life story and answering some questions he and Ellie had about my past and why I couldn't learn my powers. Ellie almost fainted when she learned how old I actually was, while Archer just looked annoyed. With this now out in the open, Archer handed me a book to read for a while to see what types of things I had ever experienced that could be magical, then we made a list and went off that to see if that was a power or just something coincidental. We figured out that so far my visions of seeing the past and the future were a power I possessed and while, unfortunately, I can't make objects do my bidding, I can go through them. "Honestly, I felt more like a spirit than a witch," I said while laughing.

"But they are unique powers," Archer said. I thought for a moment looking over at Ellie who was reading the book archer gave me.

"So, do I have the ability to change someone's future? Also, do you know how I can choose when to see someone's future instead of it happening every time I touch them?"

Archer looked like he had a horrible headache from being asked way too many questions at once. His wife put the book away and left the room to come back a moment later holding a cold wrap for his head while at the same time holding a cup of tea that she made for him. After a while and a few sips of tea, he got back up and said, "One thing at a time." We all agreed that me learning how to go through objects would be the more important power to know. "You wouldn't want to get your face or head stuck in something, then suffocate to death, do you?" Archer asked looking over at me. I realized that I hadn't even thought about that.

I looked over to Ellie then, while grabbing the sides of my head replied, "No, that would not be fun," she nodded in agreement.

Archer told me to use the book he had originally given me and to put my hand through. I tried at first with words and spells but nothing was working. I tried again with just my mind and thoughts but nothing was working. I started feeling upset that I couldn't get this to work for me. Fighting back tears, I felt my face getting red with anger and then suddenly it happened, as my hand went through the book. I got so excited for a second then immediately I began to panic because I didn't know how to get my hand back out of the book. I looked over to Archer who was giving me the, "Figure it out," look. I thought very hard of how proud I felt when I got my hand to go through the book so after a moment of feeling happy and wiggling my hand, I got it free from the book.

"Yatta!" I shouted to the room as Ellie jumped up in joy and hugged her rain cloud, Archer, who stood up after a moment and walked over to the chair in the middle of the room.

He smirked as he said, "This is the next object to go through." I immediately stopped celebrating with Ellie as I looked over at the chair. This is gonna be a long day, I thought.

Chapter Twenty-Two

I finally got home just before the sunset. My body ached all over and I had a terrible scratch from where a nail got me as I was halfway through the chair. I walked up the stairs to my apartment when I saw the door was already opened. I figured it was my nasty landlord Cleatus coming to look at my nonexistent leaking sink again. I sighed in frustration thinking that I really didn't need this right now. As I walk through the door I shouted. "I don't need anything fixed, Cleatus; so you can put your clothes back on and leave." Cleatus surprisingly wasn't there but I screamed when I saw who was.

Burroughs, my aunt Abby's cat was sitting on top of my counter watching me. My favorite coffee cup was in front of him that read, "Resting Witch Face." I held my breath as Burroughs moved his paw and pushed the mug near the edge of the counter. "Burroughs, if you break that, I won't like you anymore," I said this while moving slowly as I grabbed my mop leaning against the refrigerator. I took a step towards Burroughs who hissed at me in reply then moved the mug over again where it fell in front of my eyes and shattered on the floor. "Damn you, Burroughs!" I shouted while chasing him around the room trying desperately to hit him with my mop. Just then, my aunt Abby emerged from my bedroom, looking unhappy in a bathrobe, my bathrobe! "Why are you here?" I asked with venom in my voice. The green face mask she had on looked like it was beginning to crack in places from the anger on her face.

"Well, that's some way to speak to the aunt who raised you."

I sighed in defeat looking at her, "Are you going to be staying in town long?"

She gave me a cruel smile as she answered, "Well, yes, I am looking to relocate here since Burroughs and I are constantly needing to move." She reached over to pet her cat when he hissed and scratched her hand causing her to yelp and pull her hand back. I smirked a little at the Karma. "Anyway, my dear," she said going on while covering her hand, "I will need to stay here for the time being until I can get time to find a place of my own." I looked at her stunned. Was she high? Did she forget what she had done to me last night? Did she forget that she ran Ben off? She let out an impatient sigh, "I didn't forget what happened last night, you were extremely rude and out of line speaking to me the way you did. Also, no I am not high, and I won't even humor you with a reply to the priest."

Realizing she had just read my mind I began to gather up my things and put them in a suitcase. "Where are you going?" she asked as she stepped over the broken glass of my favorite coffee cup to get water from the fridge.

I looked at her and said, "This is a one-bedroom apartment and I'm not going to sleep anywhere Burroughs can get me. I'm going to go stay at my shop until you find a place for yourself." As I went to leave, I got a swipe from the cat causing me to add, "and Burroughs."

I began the walk to my shop since it was too late for the buses. I was so worn out, sore and full of misery that I felt numb and didn't even care. My mind and body ached all over from training with Archer today and yet my heartache trumped it all. I looked up at the sky wishing Ben would hear me out, but I haven't heard from him all day. I felt like crying but I didn't even have the energy to do that as I kept myself walking. Headlights approached me and as the vehicle pulled over, I kept my eyes forward as to not let them think I was interested at all in talking to them. "Marcy, where are you going this late, honey?" hearing her familiar voice I looked to see a limo with Pixie, my darling fairy friend, standing through the sunroof.

"My aunt is in town and taking my apartment, so I'm going to the store until she is gone."

"Oh my!" She said crinkling her nose because she hated my aunt about as much as I did. "Do you want a ride?" She offered, then said below her into the limo, "Rune darling, could you pull my pants back up so we can drive Marcy to her store?"

"No, it's fine. I really need to walk tonight." I said looking up to her. I didn't want to spoil their fun and I really did want to just be alone so I wasn't lying to her.

She could see the sadness in my eyes and said, "Okay, well, call me sometime and we can go get lunch." With that, she waved and left still standing up in the limo.

Chapter Twenty-Three

"You're not even trying, Marcy!" Archer roared in my face the next day as I got my leg stuck in a tree. We were in the middle of a wooded area since this seemed like the safest place that we could practice without breaking his belongings.

"I am trying," I panted as I tried to focus on getting the rest of me out from the tree. Archer had no idea that I had slept at my store last night. He also had no idea I was stressed that my aunt was getting into my business and my robe or that my heart was in two pieces since Ben still had made no contact with me. "I'm really trying, I promise." I sobbed.

"I really hope so." He said grinding his teeth.

After twenty more minutes with no success for me to get free from the tree Archer stood up from where he was sitting on a stump. "We are done for today, and tomorrow we are going to work on using this power in self-defense."

He turned to leave and I squawked, "Archer, wait!"

He turned around sighing, "What?"

I looked at him, then at my leg still stuck in the tree. "Aren't you going to help me get my leg out?"

He smirked and turned around to leave again, waving his hand at me. "You know how to do it. So do it."

I looked at him surprised, "Are you kidding me?" He just kept walking as I yelled to him, "What if I remain stuck here all night?"

He stopped and said, looking over his shoulder, "Then I will see you tomorrow, maybe you'll be on time for once," and with that, he left.

It was getting dark and cold as I laid there on the ground, my leg still stuck in the tree. I can't believe this, I thought, I have tried every emotion I could and I still couldn't get out. Maybe it wasn't my emotions at all that made my powers work. I don't want to be here anymore, I thought shivering from the cold night. I just want to leave and start over somewhere else, I wanted to get far away from New York, my Aunt, and the church that held Ben.

I've tried so damn hard to just live a simple life hidden from the world only to have myself exposed in the woods like a fresh piece of meat. Crap, I thought as I looked around in a panic. I hope there are no wolves in this area. Did New York have wolves? Well with my luck I would find the one pack in this entire town. I sighed as I laid there still thinking about Ben. I missed him so much and I would do anything to just have time with him to explain everything. If he didn't want to see me after that then I could accept his decision and leave him be. I finally decided that he needed to hear me out. I wanted to tell him how much he means to me and that I am a witch. I fell forward realizing my leg finally fell through the tree. My shoe didn't, but at this point, the tree could have it.

I walked out of the woods victorious and shoeless in the direction of his church. When I remembered that I didn't look probably the best to go profess my love to someone since I was covered in mud and my shoe was missing, I went instead to the direction of my store. Hoping I had another pair of shoes there. I knew I kept back up clothes but I wasn't sure about back up shoes. As I approached the shop, I saw Ben sitting on the steps. He stood up as he saw me approaching. "Marcy," he breathed like he was worried that I had been attacked again or something. I walked to him and as I got close enough, he stopped me, "I just came to talk and have some questions I want answered, please." I started feeling like this was one of those, "we need to talk," moments.

My stomach was starting to hurt but I nodded and stepped around him to unlock my store. We walked in and I asked him if he wanted to sit, indicating to my desk or the couch in the back. His cheeks went a little red when I pointed to the couch but said, "No, thank you, I will stand."

I could feel my eyes stinging as tears started to build up. "So what's up?" I asked walking past him to the backroom to get food for Ira.

"I just wanted to ask what the other night was about, is that woman really related to you?" He asked me as I put the food bowl back in Ira's cage. I was about to get her water bottle but Ben had already picked it up and was handing it over to me.

"Thank you," I said taking her water bowl then answered his question. "Yes, unfortunately, she is my aunt, she has raised me since I was born."

"I see," he said, then after a long moment of silence he went on with the next question. "What did she do to my arms? I was holding you back and the next thing I know I was dropping you, and I couldn't move at all."

I could feel the rage inside of me all over again as I thought of that night and what my aunt had done and said to him, "I know she put a spell or curse on you, but I honestly don't know which one. I still haven't even mastered my own powers yet." As I said it, I watched him to see how he would take that in.

"Would you ever hurt me?" he asked in almost a sad tone.

"No, Ben. I could never hurt you." I took a step towards him and he held his ground but I could tell he wanted to take a step back.

"Then why do you and her always torture me in my dreams?" he sounded more angry than hurt as he asked.

"I swear it's not me. I can only go through objects and see someone's past and future."

He looked down at me like he was starting to believe me but then asked quietly, "How do I know you are telling the truth?" I looked up at him, then over to the vase of roses he had got for me. I picked it up and put my other hand to the side of it. I tried very hard to make my hand go through it but nothing happened.

"Give me a second," I said sounding frustrated as I couldn't get it to work.

"Marcy, please stop," he said as he made a step towards me. He sounded like he felt sorry for me and worse like he didn't believe me. "We can get you help, honey." He said as he wrapped his arms around me. I began to sob as I tried to push him away. He held me tight.

"Please," I begged, "I can do this." He stepped back and as I looked up at him, he moved my hair from my face and as he did, I felt the warmth in my heart that he still cared. The vase fell through the hand that was holding it causing it to shatter on the floor instead of what I was intending to do. He took another step back from me, surprise was all over his face.

"I'm not a germophobe either," I told him, "I just can't touch your skin or have you touch mine." I couldn't tell if he was upset or confused as I went on. "It makes me see visions of your past and future. I haven't figured out how to control it yet." He took another step back, still not talking. I began to panic that he would be outside by the time I spit it out. "I am a witch and I'm sorry I lied and hid it from you. But I swear, I would rather die than hurt you. I'm working with a warlock to learn and control my powers. Please don't go Ben; I... I love you." He finally stopped moving so I moved towards him, throwing my arms around him tight in the biggest hug I could manage. "Please don't leave, please."

I could feel his arms around my waist as he kissed the top of my head. Then he stopped and moved me out of his arms. "Thank you for answering my questions tonight, Marcy." He had a blank look on his face which caused my heart to sink.

"I asked for a transfer from the church. I will be leaving soon."

I looked up at him as he stared past me. "How soon before you go?"

"The end of the week." he replied. I could feel a tear falling from my cheek.

"How long will you be gone?" I asked, as he looked at me while using his sleeve to wipe away my tear.

"I don't know but I think staying here is not a good idea." With that said, he turned and walked out of the door.

Chapter Twenty-Four

I was making floral arrangements for a wedding the next morning as the repairmen worked on fixing my French doors. I decided that since mine were pretty much destroyed to order some that had stained glass flower designs on the windows. The men had finished installing them long before I had finished my orders. I was about to go get some lunch when the doors opened. I was a bit surprised as I stood up and smiled as she walked into the store.

"Hello Ellie, is everything alright?" She walked up to me and we hugged one another.

"I don't know, is everything alright?" I pulled out of our embrace and looked down at her confused. "I'm a woman, darling, and I can tell that something is terribly off with you." She went on as I looked away from her stare. "Look, I am rooting for you but I can only use my feminine charm on Archer for so long. He is not the most willing to help others." Boy isn't that the truth, I thought smiling a little.

"I was about to order some lunch." I said to her watching her set her purse down.

"Good, because I can't listen to your problems on an empty stomach," she sounded serious but gave me a smile.

The next hour was full of Chinese food and telling Ellie everything. When it was over, she looked at me with her mouth slightly ajar. "Holy crap!" She exclaimed causing my ears to ring. "Sorry," she quickly apologized while realized that she had just caused me pain. "It's just, wow. I need therapy after hearing all of that. How on earth have you not checked in somewhere with padded walls?" she asked this as I stood up to give Ira the rest of my food.

"I know right. It's hard for sure but I don't want to cause problems in my training."

She stood up and grabbed her purse. "Leave it to me. I will make sure Archer lets off."

I shook my head looking at her. "No, don't. I need him to be as he is. I just need to focus on leaving my personal problems at the door or tree or wherever we train."

"Very well," she said as I walked her to the front door. "I will see you this evening then, yeah?" she asked and turned around to give me yet another hug.

"I will be there on time, hopefully." We both giggled as she left.

I arrived at Archer and Ellie's house five minutes early. To which he answers the door with, "Wow, you do own a clock."

I walked past him and put my coat up. "I am ready," I stated in a determined tone.

"Very well," he stated as he shut the door behind me. As soon as I turned around, I was met with a weight to the stomach. Instantly, it knocked me to the ground. Gasping for air as I had the wind knocked out of me. Again another weight came flying in my direction. I put my hand out to stop it only to have it break as the weight went past.

I shrieked out in pain. "You should really figure this out," he said levitating another weight. "They only get heavier from here." He smirked as the next weight was shot in my direction. I finally curled myself into a ball to hear a smashing sound from behind me. I opened my eyes to see it had passed through me and it smashed the chair I had got stuck in. I smiled in the direction of Archer just to get met with another weight. It hit my shoulder and I heard my collar bone snap.

I screamed, "Stop it, Archer!" I was in so much pain that I could feel the room spinning.

"Well, you are going to have to make me." He said as he levitated another weight to throw in my direction.

Seeing it coming this time, I rolled out of the way as it smashed into the bookshelf and as I got myself up, I put my good hand out and shouted to him, "Enough, Archer!" Fire winds suddenly surrounded him and he put his hands up to protect his face. I didn't know what was going on as I wondered to myself if that was a protection spell he had cast or another power of mine that I didn't know I had. I had never been this pissed off at someone to ever see it before. I watched him kneel down and I began to panic, wondering if I had hurt him with the fire. I put my hand down, hoping it would cause the fire to diminish. "Archer, are you okay?" I said as I ran over to him not knowing how to help.

He coughed and looked at the burning circle he was standing in for a moment and replied, "I can't move. What did you do to me?"

I looked around frantically, "I'm not sure. I just wanted you to stop throwing weights at me, that's all. I was angry, I am so sorry, Archer."

Instead of accepting my apology, he said, "Get the fire out." I looked at him like he was talking in a different language but I grabbed the pitcher of tea that Ellie left on the table. I ran back and threw it on the fire but it didn't go out. I then ran to the bathroom and filled the pitcher up and as I poured it on the fire again it still didn't go out. I looked up at Archer who looked like he wanted to kill me at the moment.

"I don't know how." I began to tear up.

"Control your emotions and calm down to get the fire to go away, you ditz," he said a little more impatient this time.

"Okay, I'm sorry; you don't have to be such an ass." I stood up with my uninjured hand out and began to count to ten while breathing deeply. After a few moments, he was still in the ring of fire.

"Try again." He barked at me. Gosh, I thought, he must not like when he isn't in control. I breathed in deeply and closed my eyes, ignoring all of my pain, when I heard a footstep forward. I opened my eyes to see Archer standing in front of me still looking pissed.

"Yay!" I shouted then as I jumped in victory I remembered my hand and shoulder were shattered causing me to scream out in pain again.

Archer looked at his floor then escorted me to his front door where he tried handing me my coat. As he laid it on top of my shoulders I asked, "Won't you need your coat?"

He looked at me confused, "Why would I need my coat?"

We stopped at the door as he opened it. "To take me to the hospital or something."

He laughed, "We don't go to the hospital. You can heal at home, but for now, I need to do some research on what that was." He had an excited tone in his voice as he pushed me out of his house.

"You're a buttface," I said to the closed door. I let out a sigh as I walked down his driveway.

Chapter Twenty-Five

I began my walk home. Every step I took caused so much pain throughout my body. As I walked, I began to wonder how the hell I was going to heal myself. I've never been hurt to this extent that laying down wouldn't help heal me so what did Archer mean by going home and heal. Also, what did I even do to Archer? Was the fire really from me? I remember one time at my aunt Abby's house where there was a tree on fire but I don't remember much after just her screaming at me. I just figured I was too close or playing with a lantern.

Really, the more I was thinking about it any time I thought there was something strange from my past that she had been around, I had a lot of black spots where I don't remember. I just assumed it was me blocking out that time in my life from her abuse. Since I now know that she has powers of her own maybe she caused me to forget any types of powers I was showing when I was young. I should ask her but right now I need to make it into the house without her seeing me this way.

I was almost two blocks away when I needed to sit. The pain was becoming too unbearable. I sat at a bus stop, leaning against the cold stone of the bench helped a little. I leaned my head back to look up at the stars though being in a large city like New York the stars were mostly hidden. As I looked up one of the stars moved and then had a red light blinking. I laughed as I realized it was just a plane. Pain shot through me again from laughing causing me to groan in pain.

My mind needed to get off of the pain. I needed to think of something else, anything else I told myself trying to get myself back up from the bench to finish the walk home. I watched as a car drove past me then stopped, "Marcy?" I rolled my head to the side to see Ben coming towards me. "Really brain, you picked Ben to think of instead of the pain?" I tried to stand up when he knelt beside me. I looked at his face. "Mmm, I really miss your pretty face, Ben," I said petting his hair with my good hand.

He grabbed my arm to stop me from rubbing his hair completely off. "You look like you're hurt bad, what happened?"

I just giggled like I was drunk, "I was training to be a witch."

"Good lord," he said, causing me to flinch in pain which then caused me to move and groan out in more pain from the breaks.

"Now listen, the Ben in my fantasies doesn't say good words like that because he knows it hurts me."

He looked at me confused then stood up. "Marcy, I'm real."

I shook my head back and forth, "No honey, I wish you were but you're just my dream man." I winked at him with both eyes simultaneously trying to be cute but he said nothing, "Oh come on, that was funny and you know it."

He chuckled, "Well yes, but it's not as funny when you are badly injured." He began to unbutton his shirt, as I watched I could feel my face go red as his eyes locked with mine.

"See now, I'm calling bull shit, real Ben wouldn't take his clothes off. Hell, even my dream Ben wouldn't strip for me. You're kind of like dry toast handsome."

He kept looking at me as a smile tugged at the corners of his mouth. "I'm using it as a sling for your arm."

"Oh," I replied feeling embarrassed as he tied my arm up to help it not move.

"Where are you heading, injured like this, anyway?" he asked while walking me to his car.

"I'm going to my house to heal myself."

He stopped walking, "You can heal people?"

I shrugged my one good side, "How the hell am I supposed to know? That's just what I was told, but a bath sound so good right now, so I thought I'd try that first." He helped me into his car and asked for my address. I told him where I lived and we headed in that direction.

"I really think you need to go to a hospital." he said, looking over at me as I tried to reposition myself to get more comfortable.

"I can't, but if my aunt is still at my place, I will more than likely end up going to the morgue when she finds out how I got injured."

Out of nowhere, the car came to a sudden stop causing me to fly forward and groans out in pain. Ben turned his whole body to look at me like I was insane. "Your aunt, the lady from your store, is at your place?"

"Yes sir, she is staying there until she can find a place of her own. I'm staying at my shop until she is gone but I need to go there to take a bath to help me and the shop's massive sink doesn't count."

He looked ahead then put the car in drive, turned around, and changed our direction. "I'm not taking you home to that lady. I will take you to the home I'm staying at. It has a very large tub and shower."

I looked out the window of the car leaning my head on the glass, too hurt and tired to argue with my imagination. Seven minutes later we arrived at his place. He walked me up the stairs through his bedroom to the bathroom. He started the water looking up to me, "Do you like the water warm?"

I groaned out, "The hotter the bath, the better." He nodded then stood up approaching me.

"Sit down so I can get your shoes and socks off." He was about to kneel in front of me until he saw my smile.

"No need, my friend," I said as I kicked my sandals off exposing my bare feet that were extremely red from the cold.

"It's still March!" He said looking at me with a sour look on his face.

"What? I haven't had a chance to get another pair since the tree in the woods ate mine." Sighing, he stood me up and began to reach for my belt.

I looked up at him shocked. "What are you doing!?" He looked up at me but his hands were still undoing the belt buckle.

"I'm helping you take your clothes off. You can't take them off yourself the way you are and you're not going to take one fully clothed." I wasn't one to be ashamed of my body but when it came to Ben, even my imaginary one, I was nervous he wouldn't like what he sees. He helped me wiggle out of my pants then looking surprised, asked, "You didn't wear underwear?" (Hey I warned you guys already that you'll be lucky if I left the house with them on.)

"I was running behind this morning," I replied starting to blush.

"But it literally takes less than a minute..." He cut himself off realizing that telling me this was probably gonna go nowhere. "Never mind," he said as he removed his shirt from around my body then told me to hold my injured arm with my good hand.

While I was doing that, he reached into his front pocket and pulled out a knife. "Wait, Ben, wait. Let's just think about this for a minute. I'll tell you anything you want to know just don't hurt the shirt!" I said backing up.

He finally smiled as he stepped towards me, "Look, lady, the shirt has to come off and if you are wearing a bra, which will be a surprise to both of us, I'm sure. I will need to cut that off too because we can't get them over your injured arm." I let out a whine but gave in and let him cut me out of my clothes. Once I was all the way exposed, I got into his enormous tub. I was afraid to sit back but I felt a little better, feeling weightless in the water.

Once I was settled in the tub, I looked over to Ben to see him with medical gloves on and on one knee rolling up his pant legs. "Now what are you doing?" I asked.

He looked up at me from where he was down on one knee. "I'm going to get in there with you and help you feel better." He stood up and looked so damn good in just his black pants. He stepped up to the tub then sat on the ledge behind me. "Lean back, I got you," he said in a very soft and caring tone. I leaned back a little as he held his hands on my back guiding me to lean on the back of the tub between his legs. I rested my head in his lap as he took a washcloth and got it wet to let the water pour over my injured side.

"Imagination Ben?" I said looking up at him.

"Yes?" he said still pouring water on me as gently as possible.

"Thank you for helping me with this."

"Of course, I got your six." He replied now running his fingers through my hair. It felt so damn amazing that I wasn't in pain anymore.

"Just so you know, though, we can't have whoopee because I don't want you to get kicked out of the church." I knew I was mumbling at this point but I just felt so relaxed and tired. As I could hear myself snoring, I felt his lips on the top of my head and I thought I heard him say something about the church but I didn't hear it all.

Chapter Twenty-Six

I awoke the next morning to the sun in my face. I groaned not wanting to get up and go to work. My bed felt amazing and I was so warm under my blanket. Then realizing I said out loud, "This is not my bed." I felt movement behind me as a hand slid on top of the covers just above my hip.

"I know, it's my bed." Ben's voice rough behind me caused me to jump. His hand on my hip gripped down as he said, "Easy, Marcy, easy." I rolled over to see Ben laying there. He smiled at me causing me to smile back until I saw that he had no shirt on and from the feel of it I didn't either.

"Excuse me a moment," I said holding a finger up then rolling away from him to look under the covers confirming that I was indeed naked. I rolled back towards Ben his grin was larger this time. I was at a loss for words so I stated awkwardly to him. "So… I'm kinda naked." He laughed in response.

I was starting to get upset as he continued to laugh at my nakedness. "Why are you laughing?" I asked as he still went on chuckling.

"Well, for starters, you are a little more than kind of naked. Then there is the fact that you thought all night that I was your Imagination Ben. Oh, and the cherry on top is that you can heal yourself with water." He began to roll away from me to face the other way.

Not knowing what else to do I looked at him starting to feel like crying. "I'm sorry, Ben."

He stopped moving, "Why are you sorry?"

I wiped my eyes. "Cause your first time was with a hippo!" I sobbed harder he moved the hair from my face.

"Marcy, we didn't do anything, see?" He flipped the covers back to expose both of our bodies. I was completely naked but he had sweat pants on.

"Oh." I sniffled, now feeling like an idiot.

"Listen," he said exhaustively while putting on medical gloves on so he could touch me, which was the reason he rolled away from me. "I know you don't think highly of yourself, but I think you are beautiful, smart, and funny." I looked away as he went on. "I like you very much."

As I looked at him, I couldn't help but ask, "Are you still leaving in a week?"

He looked at me and replied, "I am, but for other reasons." He began to touch my shoulder blade, touching as gently as possible at the healed skin while eyeing the area like a kid in science class. "Amazing, absolutely amazing," he breathed grabbing the blankets to pull them up over our bodies. He locked his eyes with mine as he reached around me to rub my back.

I was still sniffling like a ding dong but I had to know. "Will you ever come back?"

He was careful as he wiped away one of my tears, "I might visit some of the church members once in a while."

He went back to rubbing my back as I asked, "Will you ever want to visit me?"

His arm stopped and he looked a bit sad, "I suppose it depends."

Not liking that answer or the silence after it, I pushed him a little, "on…" He propped himself up on an elbow and laid his other hand on my hip as he glanced up at the ceiling.

"On, for starters, if I can talk to the higher-ups of the church in order to see if I can be with you in a romantic way." He looked down at me then went on, "There is talk of letting us date and get married but nothing has been set in stone yet for any of us." I felt my face get a little red as he smiled and ran his fingers up my side to just beneath my breast. "Then there is the matter of us figuring out how to touch without you passing out or having visions as you said."

I looked at him a bit confused as I asked, "Do you need to leave for that though?"

He smiled a wicked smile as he moved his hand from where it was to my lower back, pulling me to meet his hips. "Well, as you can tell, I do really want to touch you." I gasped in surprise feeling his "want" for me through his sweat pants. "Then the last and most important matter at hand," he said as he pushed me onto my back and at the same time pulling himself on top of me. He looked at me for a moment moving a strand of hair from my face to tuck behind my ear. I was shaking at the feel of him as he moved his right leg to rest between mine. "Are you a good witch?" As he asked this, he moved my legs apart with his while lowering his head to whisper in my ear, "Or are you a bad witch?"

I could feel my body rising up to meet his. "Can't I be both?" I whispered as I began to rub my hips against his. He let out a groan and grabbed my hair with his hands.

"Don't start something we can't finish," he growled in my ear as he pushed himself harder on me so I could feel his pain.

"You could keep the gloves on," I said as I reached under the blanket to stroke him. He pushed himself harder into my hand closing his eyes as I wrapped my fingers around him to feel every bit. He suddenly stopped and grabbed my wrist while pushing himself off of me.

Not knowing what I did wrong, I laid there for a moment, trying to read his face. After a moment of nothing, I felt like I had hurt him. "Ben, I'm sorry." He opened his eyes and looked at me finally.

"Don't be sorry I just want to do this the right way." I finally felt like I could breathe after he said that.

"So I didn't hurt you?" I asked. He smiled and kissed my side from on top of the blanket.

"You didn't hurt me at all. But we should get you dressed and back to your home before you get me thrown out of the church." I got up from the bed and saw the bathroom door open and as I looked on the floor, I saw my clothes or should I say the shreds of what were my clothes.

"Huston, we have a problem," I said looking over to Ben who was putting a shirt on.

"Well, I didn't have a whole lot of options since you broke your collar bone." I looked at him then my clothes again.

"I hope you are not taking me home naked then." He stopped what he was doing and began to look me up and down. "Ben!" I shouted.

He laughed, "I wasn't going to. Calm down." Then he handed me a long black coat.

"What's this, a trench coat?"

"No," he said, "it's a priest coat, and it should do the job till you get home and can change."

Within ten minutes we were dressed and sneaking out to his car. We got in as I looked around nervously, he grabbed my wrist and said, "It's fine, no one saw us." I sighed as I put my seat belt on. He took me home, and as we sat in his car,

I looked over at him, "Do you want to come in with me?"

He looked at my place with anger in his eyes then said to me, "Every part of me wants to, but it's best that I didn't." He looked at me and sighed. "I don't want her to hurt you because of me." I nodded in agreement and got out to head up to see the devil and her cat.

Chapter Twenty-Seven

I walked up the stairs to my apartment wondering if clothes were really a necessary thing for me at this point. I could rename my shop the "Garden of Eden" and have the first nudist flower shop in all of New York. I'm sure it would be a hit, I thought as I unlocked my door. I didn't see my aunt though as I came in, just Burroughs who welcomed me with a hiss and a swipe of his sharp claws. Obviously, I had returned the hiss to him walking past to go to my bedroom for more clean clothes to keep at my shop. Not seeing my aunt there means not having to get into any kind of argument with my aunt, which would be amazing given the night I had. Maybe she is out looking for her own place I wondered to myself as I opened the door to my bedroom. As soon as I did, I let out a scream that I had never even heard myself before. Death wasn't even this horrible in my visions, I thought, still screaming at the top of my lungs. Nothing in my entire three hundred plus years of existence had prepared me for this traumatic scene.

There, on my bed, MY BED! Was my aunt Abby and she was nude. Yes, I know that doesn't sound as traumatic to scream bloody murder since she is staying at my place and I am not. But it gets worse, so you should really sit down. There in the bed, naked with my aunt, was my sleazy landlord Cleatus. Now, I've seen both of them naked at separate times in my life, but to see them naked and mid hump, I instantly fell backwards out of my bedroom kicking the door shut with my feet. Then as I sat on my ass looking at the door in horror, I didn't even feel nausea as I just threw up all over my lap and carpet. I rolled over coughing as some of the vomit went into my lungs. Realizing that Burroughs had jumped off of the kitchen counter to come over and watch me die on the floor. I glared at him as he hissed. "Why the hell didn't you give me a heads up, Burroughs? Or at least hand me the bottle of bleach from the counter as I walked by so I would burn my eyes out of my head from that!?" He chose not to humor me with even a hiss for an answer as he began to lick his paw.

"Oh Marcy, would you get up and stop acting so childish?" My aunt was wrapped in my bathrobe standing in the doorway of my room with Cleatus standing behind her in a bath towel. His arms wrapped around her.

"Are you kidding me, I think I had the very appropriate reaction to walking in to... That!" I indicated to them with my hand. My aunt looked furious as she stepped over my vomit to go get a bottle of water from the fridge.

"You could have knocked," she said as she threw a roll of paper towel at me to clean up my mess.

"Oh, I'm sorry I forgot to knock on my own damn bedroom door. How stupid of me." I snarled back at her, cleaning up the vomit while Cleatus stood there watching us argue with a smirk on his face and his towel beginning to stand up in the front. I looked at him disgusted and encouraged myself not to throw up again.

Once it was clean, I stood up and told my aunt that I needed to get more clothes to take to my store. She finally lost her resting "witch" face and told Cleatus to get dressed so they could get some lunch. "She should be gone by the time we get back and we can resume our negotiations."

I looked at her about to say that she was not resuming anything until the last part registered in my brain. "Negotiate what, exactly?"

She turned around while getting dressed causing me to envision scratching my eyes out with sharp pencils. "I am looking into a place here to live; we are negotiating a price for a two-bedroom apartment."

I was so confused at this point that I didn't even care that they were both naked again in front of me. "Why do you need two bedrooms?"

She turned to him and said with a smirk, "Well, the negotiation is also if we want to share a one-bedroom or live in a two-bedroom." As she finished speaking, he walked by and swatted her rear. And I gagged out loud causing my aunt to glare at me.

"Ya know what?" I asked while gathering as many items of clothing as I could so I never had to come back here again until my lease was up. "I am so happy for you both and I hope you guys figure it out." Giving one last look at the place to see if I had missed anything or how much of my stuff needed to be burned, I turned around and left.

I got back to my shop and began to move everything around in the back to make it my new living area. Once finished, I let out a sigh of relief when my phone played the Witchy Woman ring tone by the Eagles. I glanced down at my phone to see that Pix had sent me a text. "Marcy, I have had a very bad feeling of distress today. I hope it's not you that is in distress. If it is then please call me ASAP. If I don't hear from you by the end of the day, I will send Horace to do a wellness check and you remember how well that went last time I sent him lol!" I smiled looking down at my phone remembering how badly that went when Horace was sent to check on me and ended up getting himself tangled in my ceiling fan because he decided to swipe a very beautiful long pearl necklace from an older socialite. I quickly replied back, "Don't send the bird, I am okay. I just wish I was born blind because I saw my aunt and my landlord having whoopee." Before I even put my phone away, Witchy Woman played out again. I glanced down at her reply of the emoji face vomiting. I replied back to her very appropriate response with, "true story!"

Chapter Twenty-Eight

The past week of focusing on my power training with Archer, living in my store, and seeing Ben in secret was actually the best week I have had in a very long time. My training was starting to excel as we trained with the fire part outside and used my going through objects power inside. However, while we were pushing on with my training, Archer and I were still curious as to why I hold such strong and rare powers. Unfortunately, we have not had much luck finding anything even close from his books on our kind. He even went as far as having Ellie surf the internet as he went through scrolls he found in Egypt on witches while on their honeymoon many years ago.

"Okay, so here it says the first witch in our history was Massika, a handmaid to the first female pharaoh MerNeith. During the night Massika would dream of Heka who is the Egyptian God of Magic and Medicine. Heka saw her as a beautiful woman even as a slave, he was also flattered that she dreamt of him. He, in turn, made her his lover and gave her divine powers of her own. She became a powerful snakecharmer which, back then, was the equivalent of a witch, but her power brought fear to many high Priests and other snakecharmers. She was so powerful that she could walk through the walls of the palace; as well as bring her pharaoh's enemies to their knees by using fire she pulled from the desert against them."

"Sounds about like you," he said looking up from the scroll to me. I was in the middle of trying to get my arm through a statue they had placed in the middle of the library when I glanced over at Ellie who nodded in agreement.

I dropped my arm out of the statue to go over to where they were sitting. "Okay, but other than her, there isn't anyone?"

"Not that I could find," Ellie said glancing back at the computer screen as a new notification popped up showing that another murder happened at a church.

"Look at this, darling," Ellie said to Archer as she pointed to the screen of the computer. He walked over as she continued speaking to him. "That is the same orange cat that was in the photos of the other church murders. That can't be a random thing." She looked up at him as he nodded in agreement.

"Perhaps you are right," he said as he read the article out loud. "Preacher Abraham died early this morning, he was found dead in the church's fountain. This is the third death of a church leader in New York causing concern as to who is responsible."

We sat in silence for a while before I asked Archer, who was now looking at the scroll again, "So what happened to Massika?"

As I looked at the scroll over his shoulder, he could feel my presence in his personal space and stood up looking at the scroll. "It says that a few of the high priests got together and planted doubt of her calling her a danger to the pharaoh so out of fear of getting overturned, the pharaoh banished her from the city."

He said as he kept reading to himself as Ellie and I looked at each other and then at him wondering if he was going to finish the story. "Then what!?" We both asked almost shouting at him in unison.

He spun around, "Oh right, sorry," he said. "It says that she survived living in the desert by controlling the land and its creatures. Heka led her to a land where they could be together and it stops there."

I sat there stunned for a moment before replying, "That's it? She didn't burn the city down or anything? She just walked away?" Archer shrugged as he looked to his wife who also sat there looking a bit defeated like me.

"Well, damn, what do we do then?" she asked looking at her husband.

"We will just continue to train Marcy and hope she doesn't burn our house down." We all laughed at that.

Then Ellie asked him, "Does this mean that Marcy is a very powerful witch?"

He snorted, "Hardly, but she doesn't have her powers mastered and she probably has more that she doesn't even know about. If she was brought up as a witch then yes, she would definitely be a powerful one to watch out for."

I thought that one over for a moment wondering if my mom had been a very powerful witch and that's why she was on the very first round of witches to die. Then I thought of my sister Dorothy. Was she powerful and not know it like me or did she get someone to teach her and she is powerful? I could go and ask my aunt Abby but I will not set foot in that building while I know those two are shaboinking. So it seemed I may have to make another trip to Salem and hope to hell that Tituba isn't very busy.

"Well, I better go home and get some sleep," I said as I stood up and stretched.

"I agree," he said holding his hand out for Ellie. She took his hand and stood up standing next to him. "Tomorrow we will do more self-defense." I groaned a no as he finished his sentence. "Oh, quit your bitching," he said in an exasperated tone. "We both now need to do self-defense training, so don't feel like it's just you."

I looked at him a bit confused and was about to ask but Ellie beat me to it. "Is she really going to be that dangerous when she masters her powers?"

He kissed her forehead as he looked down at her. "She will be dangerous, no matter what at this point." That hurt to hear, I thought to myself but I think he read it on my face because he went on. "Right now you are the equivalent of a small child. You don't have control or full knowledge of your powers so that is a danger. Then, when you do master it, since we have not come across anyone else like you, except someone from ancient Egypt time that was a powerful being, you could become dangerous and I want to know how to guard my family against you."

I got a bit defensive when he made me sound like a threat so I turned around to face him to see he already had Ellie behind him. "I would never hurt anyone, I'm not a mean person," I said a bit pissed, causing Archer to put his hands up in a surrendering motion.

"You are taking what I'm saying, wrong, Marcy, I never said you were evil but when push comes to shove, I want to keep what I have alive. Also, you may not be evil but in the world, there is always someone out there who is and any enemy of yours will obviously become an enemy of mine."

I softened up a little when he explained that to me and he was right. I would do the same thing in his position. I felt bad especially since he is doing so much to help me including sending his children away instead of spending time with them during their spring break. "I will see you tomorrow then, for self-defense lessons." My magic kicked in as I fell through his front door and hit the bottom of his porch steps hard. Ellie ran to help me up while Archer stood in the doorway. "Girl, if you had a brain, you'd be dangerous," he said laughing as I stood up thanking Ellie for helping me, then flipping him the bird as I walked away.

Chapter Twenty-Nine

I got to my shop early to get a head start on my work. I was beginning to struggle with work, witch lessons, and avoiding my aunt like the plague. I needed a break from this crap I thought, as I was putting together some bouquet of roses for a wedding, when I got an email from Ellie. I clicked on the closed envelope to see that tonight's lessons had to be cancelled due to their children getting sick as soon as they got back home this morning. "Sweet!" I shouted out loud turning in a circle to head to the back of the shop. I quickly packed my things to take a three-day stay in Salem. "This has to give me enough time with Tituba," I said to myself getting excited to learn more about who I am and what I can actually do.

I took a quick glance around the room to make sure I hadn't forgotten anything. Food and water for Ira (check), Plants all watered (check), a bag of clothes and flip flops (check, and yes I know I really need to stop and get some shoes so I don't die from the flu). I got my bag in my car and went back up the step to lock the door. I left a love note on the door for customers reading, "Life sucks, needed a break! Sorry for the inconvenience."

I got into my car as I was about to put it into the drive, my phone chimed, "Jesus wants a hug!" Boy, that hurts like a bitch every time my phone says Jesus wants a hug, but it's so damn funny that I take the pain. It was Ben's ringtone and I picked it up before it went off a second time. "Here I am, what were your other two wishes?" I asked and after a few moments, I heard him chuckle.

"Nice pickup line," he finally said then asked, "Does it work?"

"You bet your ass it does!" I said and we both laughed.

"So what's a pretty lady like you up to today?" he asked in a teasing tone.

"I am going on a road trip to Salem for the weekend."
"Oh, what's in Salem?" he asked.

I couldn't resist as I said, "My eight part-time boyfriends."

He was silent for a moment then as he realized it was my sarcasm he chuckled, "Well, I hope you are going there to let them all go since you're mine now." My heart leapt for joy at his words.

"Well, I was gonna keep one," I laughed, "but I guess I'll just have to dismiss them all." I was curious as to why he called. "Was there a particular reason you called or are you trying to sell me crap?" I asked jokingly.

"I have the next few evenings off so I wanted to see if you'd like to have dinner with me."

Awe, I so badly wanted to squeak like a teenage girl. "Then come with me." My smile was so big, waiting for him to reply.

He was quiet on the other end, then after a moment said, "Why not, let's do this." I turned my car around to head in his direction.

"Great, pack a bag and I'll see you shortly," I said then hung up on him before he could change his mind.

The drive there was full of laughter and music. It was the best time I've had in a very long time. He would pick a song that we would sing and listen to, then I would have a turn. The drive seemed to take no time at all as we arrived at the hotel just outside of Salem past 9 pm. I got us checked into the hotel as Ben got our bags. I opened the door to hear him behind me say, "Ya know, I always figured my first time in a hotel room with a girl would lead to sex beyond my wildest dreams." Then he laughed while kicking the door shut with the back of his foot before dropping the bags to the floor.

I couldn't help but smile at that, "Well, if it helps, I figured my first time in a hotel room with a guy would lead to sex, period." I turned around to give him a wicked smile only to see a blur coming at me. I gave a surprised scream as Ben lifted me up, holding me by my hips.

He trailed kisses from my chest to my stomach. "Damn, I wish I could take your clothes off and kiss your skin," he growled in my face as he pulled my hair back exposing my neck. "I want to bite you so hard here." I gulped as he laid me down on the bed putting himself on top of me.

"Ben, you know all this is going to do is frustrate us both." He gave me a smile as he lifted his head and reached into his back pocket.

"Oh geez, what do you have?" I asked eyeing him. "I brought protection!" he stated so proudly as he pulled rubber gloves from his pocket. I laughed so hard then gave a hard pass to the gloves. "But why!?" he groaned out miserably rolling off to lay next to me.

"Hey, you are the one who gave yourself an issue, not me." I sat up and looked over at him as he laid there looking at the ceiling. I leaned over and kissed his chest. "I am going to meet with a very old witch tomorrow and hopefully she can give us an answer to your problem." As I said it, I ran my fingers over the bulge in his jeans. He grabbed my wrist very tightly as he looked at me to stop. I giggled at the look of pain and hatred in his eyes. "Okay, I may have been the one to give you an issue that time."

I was having a good dream for once even though I don't remember what it was about when the curtains to the window flew open exposing the sunlight in my face. I put my hand up to guard my eyes as I hissed. "Oh stop it, you wanna be vampire," Ben said laughing. I heard him turn the shower on as I laid there trying to go back to sleep. A while later, Ben threw a damp towel on me. "Hurry up before the water gets cold," he said as I groaned in reply.

"You can go take your shower first, I'll go second," I mumbled to him finally going back to sleep.

"I already took a shower first, silly. There is only one towel so I was giving you the one I just used."

I sat up so fast my head spun around for a moment. "Oh cheese and toast." I breathed as I saw Ben, all of Ben. He was the most perfect man I ever laid eyes on. I felt like I was drooling and I'm sure I was, so I wiped the side of my mouth just to be sure.

He laughed and walked over to me. Oh shit, oh shit I thought. I was like a kid in a candy store. I want to touch everything on him even though I was told not to. He stopped in front of me then bent down to get his bag, then he turned away from me to go get dressed in the bathroom, covering his rear end with the bag. I'm an ass person so I was very angry that he wouldn't let me see. "No one likes a tease!" I shouted at him. He turned his head in my direction smirking as he was about to close the door to the bathroom. He moved the bag over to the sink giving me a glimpse of his ass that put Riley's to shame! I was left staring at the closed door wishing I had x-ray vision. Damn that man is good in more ways than I thought.

"Screw the shower, I'll take one later," I said to the closed door as I got up and began to put my clothes on. I was sitting on the edge of the bed waiting for him. Moments later, he emerged from the bathroom in blue jeans and a grey sweater that hugged him just right. It honestly left me breathless as he walked over and sat next to me putting his boots on.

He slapped my thigh with his hand as he asked, "You ready to go?" I nodded unable to say anything as he got up and walked in front of me to open the door. I thought he looked good naked but the tightness of those jeans on his rear end drove me wild. I really need to find Tituba now and get this problem resolved I thought to myself following him outside. I might just die from lack of Ben if I don't!

Chapter Thirty

After getting in the car, we made it to Salem in no time. I got out and put my gloves on. It wasn't cold enough to wear them but I was a little worried about meeting Tituba again. She was very kind but she made it known by showing me what she did that she is not to be messed with, so I might need Ben to hold my hand. I walked around to the front of the car where he was waiting for me. He reached for my hand with his and I noticed he had his gloves on too. He looked down at my hand and smiled, "Great minds think alike." We walked over to the jail where I assumed Tituba would be since there was a group going through. We made our way behind them unnoticed. As we got to the section where my mother's name was on the jail cell. I stopped to look at it and felt a tear coming down my face.

"Marcy, are you alright?" Ben asked as he rubbed my back.

"This is where I was born," I said sniffling.

I could feel Ben's hand stop as he asked, "What do you mean? How old are you?"

I looked up at him and replied, "Really, out of everything, you're worried about dating an older woman?"

He laughed, "Hey, it could be a deal-breaker. Ya never know." He leaned down and kissed the side of my head, "Come on, we don't want to lose the group," he said walking away to join the rest of the crowd.

I stood there for a moment letting out a sigh, "I wish I had a chance to meet you, to have you raise us instead of aunt Abby." I laid my hand on the bars of her cell when out of nowhere a feeling of dread came over me. I felt dizzy watching the room spin, I let go of the bar trying to find my balance and losing as blackness covered me like a blanket covering me up.

I was in her cell with a woman who I had never seen before. She was thin and her clothes were torn and dirty. I began to panic that Tituba had tricked me and now I am going to be her prisoner like the others. "How long have you been in here?" I asked walking past her as I began to shake the bars of the cell and call out for help.

She looked up at me, "Don't waste your time or strength, honey, it won't do you any good."

I spun around to face her and she looked much worse than the other girls did. "Well, we have to do something," I shouted with panic in my voice. Walking over to where she sat, then remembering the other girls in the jail were witches who turned on everyone, including other witches. I glared down at the woman and with venom in my voice, I asked, "Are you a witch?"

She looked at the bars letting out a small sigh as she said, "It doesn't matter if I am or not, I have nothing more to live for. My husband passed away before all of this and now my children are gone." She began to sob as she finished speaking. I felt sorry for a moment, I didn't have much of a family and the ones I lost were when I was small so I don't remember. I still wasn't sure if I could trust her. These women showed me the last time how good of actresses they can be.

"Again, I will ask you, are you a damn witch!?" I shouted at her. She began to cry harder. So I sighed and sat next to her. "Look, I'm sorry I yelled at you, but I'm not from around here and I can't stay here either," she wiped the tears from her eyes watching me as I stood up walking back over to the bars.

"You can't get out, none of us can." I tried to go through the bars but nothing was happening. I remembered Tituba had put a curse on them. I began to pull on the cell door when my hand slipped off the bar causing me to fall backwards.

I groaned sitting up looking around for any other solution. I began to lose hope as I pulled my knees up to my chest sitting in the straw. "There has to be a way out," I said looking at my cellmate feeling tears fall down my face. She scooted over and wrapped her arms around me.

"Shhh, do not cry, someone will come for you." She began to rock us back and forth grabbing a piece of straw and holding it between her fingers until it turned into a white flower. She showed it to me then placed it in my hands. "I was always told these mean sanctuary."

I looked at her, "These are called Queen Anne's Lace, thank you." She smiled and nodded.

"If you are a witch then why won't you use magic to get out of here?" I asked confused.

She looked at me with a sad smile. "I told you, I have no reason to live anymore." The jail door slammed open causing us both to jump. Two men in wigs entered with two guards close behind them. They stopped at our cell, pulling the door open, the guards grabbed my cellmate and dragged her over to the wigged men. I ran to the bars telling them to not hurt her. I was met with the hand of a guard. I stumbled back, trying to see where she was going.

"Sarah Good." One of the wigged men stated with a paper in front of him as the one next to him held a bible. "The town of Salem and its people have found you guilty of witchcraft and therefore, you will be taken to the gallows and hung by the neck until dead." I was frozen in place realizing that she, my cellmate, was my mother. She was so beautiful and gentle. The guards began to drag her to the door and I screamed at the top of my lungs causing the guards to drop her. I ran to the bars with tears falling from my eyes as I pleaded to them.

"Don't do this. She's a good person, she can't die, please, she is a good person!"

The men left my mom where she lay and walked over to me. "You will remain silent, witch," a wigged man said as he spat in my face.

I grabbed his robe pulling him towards me, "You are the monsters, not us." I said through the bars spitting back in his face. I didn't see the guard's hand coming at my face this time but when it made contact, it knocked me back causing me to blackout for a moment. I couldn't get back up this time as I rolled onto my side watching them pick my mom up and pulling her to the door. "I love you, mom, I am so sorry." I saw her turn her head as she heard me.

She gave me a grim smile probably thinking I got hit so hard and I was hallucinating. "I love you too, my dear sweet girl."

I could hear shouting and cheering as the townspeople were celebrating her death. I pulled my knees to my chest as I continued to cry. The crowd got quiet for a few moments, then a roar of cheer and applause as I heard the rope making a weird, almost whip noise. "Please get me out of here," I sobbed as I held my hands over my ears. "Get me out of here," I said to myself. My chest hurt so much from possibly the worst heartbreak of my life. My mother, who was a good witch, just died for nothing being nothing, and I couldn't even help her. I felt a hand on my shoulder and a voice calling my name. Knowing, no one else was in the cell with me, I began to panic.

"Marcy, honey, are you alright?" I opened my eyes to see Ben and Tituba looking down at me. I was laying on my back near the jail cell.

"You were out for a long time, I was about to go in and get you," Tituba said as Ben helped me up. "Though, I am not entirely sure that I can go into your visions," she shrugged.

I thanked Ben for helping me up and he hugged me tightly whispering in my ear. "I am very sorry to do this but there was another murder at one of the churches. They are calling a meeting for all church leaders and I must go."

I whispered back, "I understand, go." I went to let go and step out of the hug but he pulled me back in hugging me tighter.

"When you come home text me and I will come over," he said looking into my eyes, "be safe."

He turned to leave and nodded to Tituba. She looked up at him and gasped. "Arthur Shepard?" She smiled as she walked closer to Ben. "I would have sworn on everything I had that you were a normal man." She chuckled and hugged Ben around his mid-section. Ben pulled out of her hug confused.

"I'm sorry ma'am but my name is Benjamin Shepard." She looked at me and I nodded. She took a step back looking him up and down, then to me. "My word, is he the person who gives you visions?"

I looked at Ben who was staring at me. "It's okay, Ben, get back to New York and I'll see you when I'm done here." As he walked away, I looked at Tituba and said, "He was the only one I had visions of, until now, when I just had one of my mom. I was touching the jail cell when it happened."

Tituba looked at me for a moment. "Did meeting her answer your question from last time you visited?" I looked at her confused, until I remembered what she was talking about.

"Yes, she gave up," I said fighting back the tears. Tituba could see me struggling but remained quiet as she pulled me in for a hug.

Moments later we were in the servants' quarters drinking tea as I went over everything with Tituba. When I was finally finished with my story, she looked quite shocked. "That was better than any soap opera I have ever seen!" I laughed but I think she was serious. "Marcy, it is possible that you are a very powerful witch. I myself have never seen your types of powers before and I have been around a very long time." She paused for a moment then went on, "With that being said you should take caution to those around you. If your aunt finds out she will manipulate you into doing horrible things. There are many evil witches out there who can control someone who is not trained or strong enough to fight back. This Archer person training you, do you trust him?"

I thought for a moment, "He is the biggest jerk I have ever met but I trust him when it comes to magic."

She nodded standing up to walk me to her door. "Keep your circle small, Marcy, and trust no one else."

Chapter Thirty-One

I got back to the hotel room and sat down to relax. The TV had been left on from earlier when Ben wanted to check the weather. The news was on, doing a story about adopting dogs. They had some of the cutest puppies on there that I thought about getting one when the story changed to a Breaking news bulletin. The lady at the scene was very pretty, wearing a navy blue pea coat and had long dirty blond hair. "Good afternoon, I am Lorelei Margaret. I am standing at the new hope church right here in Queens, NY. Police say that a reverend at this church was found dead from choking on his blood in the sanctuary of his church." I dropped the glass I was holding causing it to shatter all over the floor. The news reporter went on, "This is the fourth church killing in this area since February. Local authorities are unsure if these killings are related to religion, random hate, or something mythical beyond our knowledge. For more on this story, see the news at nine. I'm Lorelei Margaret."

I sat on the edge of the bed stunned with my hands covering my mouth. I couldn't believe how many higher-ups in the church were being killed. I didn't really think about it until now. Are they targeting at random or is it some sort of hit list? Was Ben on that list? It's why he was brought here, to begin with. As I was lost in thought I heard my phone chime, "Every Party needs a party pooper that's why they invited you!" I glanced down already knowing it was Archer's ringtone. I hit the F-you button sending him to my voice mail. I heard a knock at the door and I stared at it for a moment. Then wondering if Archer had a tracker on my phone, I took it out, glancing it over as I walked to the door.

As I opened it, Tituba entered, surprising me. "Tituba, is everything alright?" I asked as she sat in a chair.

"No, we have a very big problem." I blinked for a moment as she sat there looking at her hands.

"I will put the tea on then," I said as I walked over to the sad excuse for a kitchen. I handed her the tea and sat in the chair across from her with my own cup.

"So, what's wrong?" I asked taking a sip of the tea and burning my tongue.

"There are murders going on around your home."

I looked at her as I gently placed the cup on the middle table, smiling I replied, "You do know I live in New York, right? It's full of murders."

She gave me an exhausted look as she replied, "You know what I am referring to, Marcy. The men being killed are in the churches."

"Okay, what about them?" I asked picking my cup back up for a second round of burning my tongue. She showed me the news bulletin on her phone to show the picture of a dead body under a sheet that was soaked in blood. "OMG, Tituba, really!?" I yelled as I spat my hot tea on my lap, which, by the way, didn't cool it down any.

"Look, Marcy!" she said showing me the photo again.

"But I don't wanna look," I whined because I didn't want to see a dead body even if it was covered with a sheet.

After a moment, I finally looked at her phone. I didn't see anything weird, just the body in front of the altar. Making sure I didn't miss anything I glanced at it again before looking at her, "Okay, so?"

She sighed, "The cat, Marcy, that Cat!" I looked back at her phone and sure enough, by the altar was a light orange cat. Then as I began to think back to the other murders at a church, they all had two things in common. The guys were leaders of the church and that orange cat was always there.

"It's got to be a different cat, these murders happened in different parts of the city," I said to Tituba who was all but laying her face on the phone to get a better look at the cat.

"You don't even believe that." She said still looking very closely at her phone. "I can read your thoughts remember?"

I sighed in frustration. "Why is this such a big issue? It's not like the cat is a whi…" Just like that, it hit me. Tituba finally got off of her phone long enough to confirm my thoughts. "A witch is doing this to the leaders of churches?" I asked in shock almost dropping my tea.

"Yes, but I have not seen this witch before and I know about every one of us," she replied going back to the photo. My phone chimed, "Jesus wants a hug!" causing us to both flinch in pain.

"I'm so sorry, Tituba," I said apologetically trying to fish my phone out from my pocket before it said it again. "Hello?" I answered standing up and walking over to the window to get better service.

"Hey you, just thought I would check-in and see how it's going." He was so damn sweet, it almost made my teeth hurt.

"Well, it's um… going." I didn't know if I was allowed to say anything to him about the cat or the possible witch behind it.

I glanced at Tituba who was back to looking at the photo on her phone. "Marcy?" I'd forgotten for a moment that he was still talking to me.

"I'm sorry, Ben, the service in here is bad. What did you say?"

"I said I miss you." he said quietly that I felt obligated to whisper back, "Awe, I miss you too. Why are we whispering?" He laughed and replied in his normal volume, "I just got done going over things here with the heads of the church. They were walking past me when I said it." I had forgotten that our relationship was a secret due to his status at the church.

"What was the meeting about?" I asked watching Tituba stand up and came over to where I was.

"It was about how to protect ourselves and our church members."

"Ask him if the police gave them more information than they gave the news?" She was practically on top of me, so I walked a few steps away as I asked.

"All they gave us that isn't on the news is the exact locations of the deaths, but anyone can google the churches and get the same thing."

"Did the police mention anything weird about the crime scenes?" I was hinting at the cat.

"Just that each death was a form of torture, and the pastor who fell from the top of his church was actually not a suicide but a murder as well. When they showed us photos of the bodies, I noticed that he had rope burns on his wrists." I heard voices in the background, then Ben said he needed to go into another meeting.

I hung up the phone, looking at Tituba, who just looked at me in return. "What do we do now? How do we prevent this from happening again?" I asked hoping she knew what to do, cause I sure as in the hell didn't.

"I have never come across this before. I will have to get our counsel together and see what they think needs to be done."

I started laughing as she finished speaking, "You guys have a counsel?" I kept laughing holding my ribs in pain. "What do you guys do? Meet witches from New Orleans and brew a pot together?" She didn't find any of that humorous and kept glaring at me so I quit laughing immediately.

"For your information, we have witches all across the world, and we get two members from each country to meet for our counsel." Well, I felt like an ass hat for offending Tituba.

Tituba smirked at my facial expression, knowing I felt bad, then stood up and walked towards the door, "I must leave, but I will let you know if I find anything out, and let me know if you find anything out too." I nodded as I walked behind her. She stopped at the door and turned to me. "I will see you tomorrow and don't forget what I said. Trust no one." I gave her a hug and let her know what time I would come and see her tomorrow.

I sat down to hear my voicemail from Archer. "Marcy, where are you? We need to train more. If you died somehow, I can't say that I'm surprised, but if you are just faking so you don't have to practice, I'm going to be really mad." I could hear shouting in the background and Archer let out a sigh

"Ellie said hi," then he hung up. I sighed as I took my shoes off and snuggled into my bed. I had a lot to process but honestly, I couldn't focus much on my problems when I couldn't stop thinking about how my mom just gave up in the end. She had so much to live for and she just let go. I rolled onto my side feeling the spot on the bed that Ben was laying on last night. I laid there I wished he could be here. I really wanted to talk to him and have him hold me the way he does best when I fall apart. I settled for the pillow he slept on but the smell of him like everything else in my life right now was not there, no matter how much I wanted it to be.

Chapter Thirty-Two

I woke early the next morning to get ready to check out. I jumped into the shower and as soon as I was dressed, I packed Ben's belongings first because he left so quickly yesterday. A photo of him in his military days fell from the bottom of his bag. He was in the photo with four other men standing in front of a military Humvee. I picked it up to get a closer look at him. He was smiling from ear to ear next to his buddies. I couldn't help but smile at his happiness. Then I gently put the photo back in the bottom of his bag. After I packed and loaded up my car, I drove over to Tituba for one last meeting.

She greeted me at her servants' quarters. I walked in and we exchanged very little information on the case. While we were talking, my phone vibrated in my back pocket. I looked at it and was thankful I put it on vibrate. It was Ben. I picked it up putting it on speaker, "Hello, you're on the air."

As soon as he was done laughing, he replied, "Hey, I'm Ben. Long-time listener, first-time caller."

I gave a chuckle then it was time to be serious. "What's up, buttercup?" I asked.

"Just called to check on you and make sure you are doing alright."

I looked over to Tituba as I said, "Yes, I'm doing good, how about you?"

"I'm fine, are you coming home tonight?" he asked in a deep tone causing the hairs on my arms stand up.

I cleared my throat and said, "Yes, but that's all you need to know right now since when I say you are on the air, it means you are on speakerphone where others can hear you."

We were all quiet for a moment then he said, "Copy that!"

I hung up with him and told Tituba that I needed to leave shortly because Archer was still blowing up my phone for lessons and I can only fake my death for so long. "Before I go, Tituba, I would like to see if you can tell me more about my visions when I touch Ben."

She looked at me, "As far as?"

I sighed, "As far as, is there any way to stop it even for short periods of time?" I stared at Tituba as I waited for her answer.

She finally got up and grabbed a book from her den. She brought it back, handing it to me. I glanced at it while she spoke, "It would seem that you have a bonding power with this man. What I handed you is a journal from the days after your birth during the trials," she took the book for a moment, opening it to a certain page then she handed it back to me.

I looked at the page reading it. "17th July 1692. Sarah Good is recovering well after delivering a premature daughter. The child named Mercy is showing much strength for being so small."

"Is this Arthur Shepherd?" I asked looking up from the book to Tituba, who nodded. I continued reading the next page.

"18th July 1692. The child survived the night still thriving. Leaders notified me that the mother will be hung tomorrow. Bringing Phillis here this afternoon to speak to Sarah about options for the two girls. An agreement was made to Sarah, Phillis and I tried to persuade the leaders to let us take the older child of Sarah to a church well known for helping children. Unfortunately, we were denied request for taking the child. Just before midnight, Phillis and I entered Jail. I got older daughter, Dorcus, out and in the wagon, I then went back in to talk to Sarah while Phillis took infant baby, wrapping the child in her cloak and going to wagon to sit with children. Sarah asked that we take the children to her sister. We left the town of Salem in the night to deliver children to a safe home. Back before sunrise, where leaders asked what had happened to the daughters. I notified them that the infant died in the night due to jail conditions and older daughter must have escaped."

I finished reading, looking at Tituba for a moment. "Okay, so I have a special connection with Ben because his family saved me as a baby, he makes my heart dance, and he's fine as hell. How can I prevent my visions from happening every time we touch?"

Tituba smiled and asked, "Did you not open the box I gave you last time you were here?"

I blinked for a moment trying to remember what she was talking about. Then it came to me, "Oh crap." I said standing up. "This whole time I had something that could have helped?"

Tituba smile and said, "That's why I gave it to you, Marcy." She stood up to walk me out.

"In my defense, I thought it was someone's heart, or worse." She laughed, though I was serious.

I made it to the car and sent Ben a text letting him know I was headed back. "I have some great news from this last meeting. Come over to my place and I will tell you what it was about." I replied back that I would see him soon excited to see what the meeting was about, but more importantly I was excited to see him. I made the drive in a little under four hours. I will neither confirm nor deny that I was speeding but I really wanted to go home and see Ben. My phone chimed while I was driving and it was Archer. I finally picked it up and answered, "I'm alive, it's a miracle!"

I heard him telling his wife to get in the car. "You're not funny, Marcy, we need to practice. Be at my house in one hour or find yourself another teacher."

I know Archer is a dick but I have never heard him upset like that before. I must have that effect on men, I thought. I made a turn driving in the direction of my home to get the box Tituba gave me. Wondering while headed that way if there was a spell that could make me blind. Ya know, just in case.

Chapter Thirty-Three

I ran up the stairs to my apartment feeling crunched for time; as I reached my door, I knocked loudly then unlocked it. No one was home that I saw so I yelled out, "I need to get something out of my room, please don't be naked!" There was no answer, so I entered my bedroom to get the box from my bag where I forgot about it. I studied the box for a moment looking at the wood carving of a weeping willow tree on the top. I walked towards my bed and sat on the forest green bench in front of it. I tucked my feet up under me as I laid the box down facing it. I held my breath as I was nervous to see what was in the box. "Okay, don't scream," I said to myself as I opened the lid.

Inside were two beautiful rings. One ring had a beautiful white stone in the center with a phoenix on one side of the ring and an Egyptian cross the Ankh on the other side. The other ring had a black stone in the middle with a flower on one side and a triangle on the other side. A note was on the top of the rings from Tituba. "Marcy, I am giving you these two rings to let you decide which to use. The ring with the white moonstone has the power to control emotions of others as well as give spiritual growth to yourself; it can calm and balance you with your powers to better control them." Crap, I thought picking the ring up to look at it. Archer would be so pissed if he knew I had this for a while. I placed the ring back down and continued reading. "The other ring has a black moonstone which gives the power to change yourself and the environment you're in. This ring can change your difficulties in life for the better." I looked at the black moon ring, thinking how messed up my life is now and how I desperately wanted my old one back. "I hope you pick the right one for you, so you can give the other to one in need." What did she mean by giving it to someone in need?

I stood up, looking at my watch, stressing that I was going to be late. I put the box on my dresser, making my way to use the bathroom before I went to training. My phone chimed and as I glanced at the message from Archer, "You better be here on time because we are leaving." I smirked as I went to text back, "Okay, okay, don't get your panties in a bunch." As I went to hit send knowing that was going to make him angry, I slipped and fell on the floor of the bathroom hitting the back of my head. "That didn't hurt or anything." I groaned from the pain, thinking that was beyond instant Karma for the text. I sat up angrily to see why the floor was so wet and who wanted to get yelled at for it.

There was blood everywhere and as I began to feel myself shake, looking at my hands that now had blood on them and from the way my back and ass felt wet, I was covered in blood. I quickly felt the back of my head, making sure I didn't crack it that hard when I fell. There was nothing on my head so I glanced at my beautiful big bathtub for a towel, that I lay over the side, only to see Cleatus dead in it. His clothes were soaked from his own blood and he had a huge hole through his stomach. I screamed, feeling all of my blood leave my face. I had never seen an actual dead body in person so I was not prepared for this.

Feeling like a child in distress, I screamed my aunt's name but she didn't reply or show up. I got myself up, trying not to slip and fall in the blood again, as I made it to the toilet just in time to throw up. I screamed her name again with more panic in my voice. I began to worry that she was hurt or dead too. I needed to search the rest of the place for her. I made it out of the bathroom and into the living area, walking and checking each room carefully. The apartment was still and silent, letting me know she was nowhere to be found, I couldn't even find Burroughs. I ran back into my room and grabbed the box heading downstairs to my car.

I grabbed my phone, dialing Pixie as I put the car into gear, heading to Archer's house. "Marcy?" she answered with concern in her voice. "I was about to call you, I am feeling extreme fear and dread for some reason. Are you okay?"

I gave a hysterical laugh as I answered, "Oh, ya know, I just went to my place to get something and found Cleatus in my bathtub."

She made a gagging sound, "You may have to take your aunt's advice and knock on the doors before you end up gouging your eyes out, on top of needing intense therapy."

I couldn't get the horrible image of Cleatus with a massive hole through his stomach, out of my head. I tried not to throw up in my car as I replied, "No, Pixie, Cleatus was in my tub, dead." There was a long pause before she said anything that I was worried we lost connection.

"What do you mean he is dead?" she finally asked as I pulled my car over to the side of the road. I opened the door and threw up, not able to hold it in anymore. "Marcy, what do you mean he is dead in your tub?" Pixie sounded about how I felt.

"I went home to get something out of my room. When I got there, I went into the bathroom to go pee and found him in my tub with a hole in his stomach and there was blood everywhere. So, like, that kind of dead in my bathtub!" My last words were full of panic.

I know she was trying to calm me down but when she said, "It's going to be okay, Marcy, everything will be fine." I pulled my phone away from my ear and stared at it like it had lost its mind. "Marcy? Are you there, Marcy?" I began to cry hysterically.

"How can you say it will be okay when my bathtub is ruined!?" I sobbed. "I loved that tub and now I'll never be able to look at it the same way again, let alone use it!" I didn't want to say the rest but felt like I needed to add, "Oh and I guess that Cleatus being dead is a bad thing too." I heard her sigh.

"I know you are not trying to be funny when someone is dead in your apartment."

The smirk on my face dropped as I realized she was right and even making a joke like that probably makes me a psychopath. "I'm sorry, I am just scared, okay, I don't know what to do."

I began to drive on the road again to Archer's house. "Where is your aunt? Is she hurt or dead too?"

I snorted, "I couldn't get that lucky, but I couldn't find her or her damn cat anywhere in the apartment. She changes phones every month so I have no idea how to get in contact with her." I felt like I was going to get sick again, trying hard to keep it down.

"Maybe she found a place of her own," Pixie said trying to give ideas. "Yeah, but why kill Cleatus on her way out? Plus, something just doesn't feel right about the whole thing." Pixie was talking to, I'm assuming Rune, in the background then said to me. "We will be at your place in about an hour to help you get this cleaned up while trying to figure out who did this."

I wanted to cry again. This girl has always had my back and I couldn't imagine my life without her in it. "Thank you, Pix."

I went to hang up when she said, "Marcy, I love you and it will be okay."
I couldn't hold my tears back anymore as I said, "I love you too, Pixie."

Chapter Thirty-Four

I arrived at Archer's to see him standing at the porch glaring daggers at me while Ellie was loading bags into their van. I turned my car off, reaching for the box from Tituba, I grabbed the white ring and put it on my middle finger. I stepped out to hear Archer telling Ellie and the kids to get back into the house until he tells them to come out. Ellie immediately obliged, walking the kids towards the house, she covered their eyes while looking at me like she'd seen a monster. I began to walk up to Archer as I did, he moved his leg back to get in a defensive stance. Geesh, I knew he would be pissed at me for being late and most likely the text too but not this pissed. "Don't come any closer, Marcy," he ordered while reaching his arm out in my direction.

I stopped putting my hands up looking at him confused, "What the hell is your problem, Archer? I know I'm a little late and yeah, the text wasn't probably that funny to you, but why are you acting this way?"

He still had his arm raised like he was going fight me as he said, "You show up to my house covered in blood and my wife got called a witch-lover today. I have done my damnedest to keep what I am, a secret to protect my family and now it's done, and it's over, so leave and never find me again."

His words hurt more than I thought it was going to as I stared watching him lower his arm and turn to go back into his house. "Archer, wait, please!" I yelled running towards him wanting to have him just hear me out. He immediately turned at me while levitating up two stone gargoyles from Ellie's garden and hurled them in my direction. I put my arm in front of my face to protect myself and closed my eyes to prepare for the impact and the pain to follow. I heard the stones slam into my car behind me I opened my eyes realizing they both had gone through me. I looked at Archer with a smile on my face. "I actually did it," I said feeling proud of myself.

"I see that," he grunted as he began to levitate a large birdbath next to him. "But it's too late for that now," he breathed out as the birdbath came hurling at me. I stood there hoping my magic would work again I flinched as it went through and smashed into my car in causing the windshield to break and the alarm to go off.

We both stood there exhausted looking at each other like an old western film. "I just need to talk to you, Archer, please, don't throw more stuff at me. I would never hurt you or your family." He glared at me while lifting his arm back up. I glanced to his sides to see what else he had to throw but didn't see anything. Then as it sunk in that the only other thing around us both was my car.

It was levitating above me as I looked at Archer who was glaring at me again. "Speak then, but when you are finished know that I will destroy your car and you under it." I could feel my eyes stinging as tears began to form. I wasn't ready to die but I was stuck at this point.

"Alright, first of all, I am sorry that I was late... again," that didn't seem to change his expression so I continued on. "I am also sorry I showed up covered in blood, I got to my house and my landlord was dead in my tub, and I slipped and fell on the floor that had his blood on it." This did change his expression.

"Did you kill him?" he asked with an eyebrow raised.

"No, of course not!" I said surprised and slightly offended that he asked me that. "He was dead when I got there. I freaked out, threw up, and then drove here."

I could feel the heat coming off of the bottom of my vehicle from when it was running. I glanced up to see that the car was lowering on me. "Why did you come to me, then?" he asked with venom in his words. "Don't you have other friends to help you hide a body?" As he asked, I felt the pressure of the car as it was now lower than before.

"I do, but I was told to trust no one else but you." I began to lower my head as the car's pressure began to crush me. You'd think I would be thinking about all of the regrets I had in life but honestly, I was getting angry that this dill weed was going to crush me with my own damaged car and not trust me.

"Get the car off of me, Archer!" I yelled to the ground, not able to stand up. "I'm telling you the truth and I am tired of you not trusting me." I must have sounded pretty angry because after a moment I could feel the car's weight going up allowing me to stand. Once it was no longer on top of me, I looked at him.

"Who told you that, who else did you tell that I was a warlock?" he asked as I felt the car start to come down on me again but I was so angry that I saw red. Electricity pulled from the car to me and I gave it all to Archer. I saw his body light up for a moment then fall to the ground. As he did, the car crashed down on me.

Chapter Thirty-Five

"ARCHER!" I awoke to Ellie screaming his name, as I opened my eyes, I was looking at the under part of my car. I'm guessing I must have dropped when Archer did, which is good because I wasn't sure if my magic was good enough to get me through a car. "Oh Archer, honey." I could hear Ellie sobbing and I tried to move my head to look but my fat was in the way so I couldn't. Did I kill Archer? I wondered as I began to feel sick. I didn't mean to kill him, I just got upset that he wouldn't listen to me. I could feel tears running down my eyes. I would never want to hurt him or his family and the way Ellie sounded I just shattered both. I took the sleeve of my sweater and rubbed my eyes and nose. There was blood all over me at this point, as I looked at my sleeve, I couldn't tell if it was even mine.

"Marcy?" Her sweet voice made me jump and I turned my head to the driver's side to see Ellie laying on her stomach. Her eyes were red and puffy from crying over Archer that I wanted to die for causing her that much pain. "Are you okay?" she asked.

I began to tear up again. "Oh Ellie, I am so sorry. I didn't mean to kill Archer."

She gave me a sad smile, "I know." I began to sob and felt her hand hold mine. "Would you stop crying, you pansy? Seriously, my kids cry less than you do." I stopped crying instantly as I watched the car lift up off from me.

I sat up and saw Archer standing there lowering my car back on the ground behind me. He looked awful but he was alive. "Who told you not to trust anyone but me?" he asked again. I sat on the ground looking at him wondering why the hell that was so important at this moment.

"I went to Salem a few times and spoke with Tituba, she is one of the originals there…"

He rolled his eyes as he cut me off mid-sentence. "I know who Tituba is." Then he limped over to where I was sitting to stand next to his wife. "So you have told no one about me then, besides her?" I thought for a moment making sure that was it, then realized it wasn't. "My fairy friend, Prudence, who now goes by Pixie, knows."

He thought for a moment before asking, "Does she have crows?" I nodded and he glared at me. "Okay, did you tell anyone not magical about me?"

I looked up to him wishing he would just believe me "No, not at all!"

He looked down to Ellie as she said to him, "I believe her." So he nodded grabbing her hand to kiss it. He took a step in my direction and I was afraid he was ready for round two. He instead lowered his hand to me. I looked at it for a moment, then up to him. He waited for a moment sighing. I grabbed his hand as he helped me up.

"Archer, I am so sorry that I hurt you," he snorted at me while still limping as he walked, "You didn't hurt me, you did shock the shit out of me though."

We made it up to his front porch where I explained everything that happened. Ellie looked horrified as I told the story and Archer, well, he looked like Archer. Once I told them he stood up and looked at Ellie. "Get all of the money out of the safe, get the kids and go."

She looked up at him confused, "Without you?" he nodded gathering her hands up in his. "Where do you want us to go, love?" she asked as she began to cry and pulled his hands up to her cheek.

"Go to our lake house in Michigan," he said gently wiping away her tears.

"Will you come once you're done?" she asked.

He kissed her forehead then her cheek. "I will be right behind you."

She hugged him tightly. "You better be," she gave a little laugh through her tears. He pulled her face up and kissed her.

She walked back into the house closing the door.

Archer looked at the door for a moment then turned to me. "Okay, let's go hide the body." I smiled, then as we turned to go down the walk, I looked at my destroyed car.

"So…" I said as he sighed and walked back up the steps.

"Ellie, I'm gonna need some of that money to get a new car for Marcy, since I kinda broke hers."

Chapter Thirty-Six

We took a taxi to my house since there wasn't enough time to go car shopping. It was a quiet ride there since Archer and I were still hurting from our epic battle (that I won, by the way).

As we were a few minutes away he leaned over and whispered, "Once I turn him to ashes, I'm leaving." I nodded in silence. Then he grabbed my hand causing me to jump. He was looking at my ring but it was still weird having him touching me.

"Where did you get this, and how long have you had it?" his tone was low and demanding.

"I got it as a gift and I've had it for a while, I just didn't know that I had it." He smirked as he dropped my hand from his, "Did you think it was a part of a body too?" I looked at him surprised. He shrugged, "Tituba was my trainer." Then he looked back out his window as he went on, "Ellie wears the white moonstone around her neck because she is my balance and calm. I would only use it in emergencies." I wondered if he wore the black one around his neck. He answered before I got the chance to ask. "The black moonstone is kept in my safe, I don't ever use it."

Once we arrived at my home, I saw Rune's Limo parked on the side with the driver and another guy standing by it. I didn't exactly live in the best neighborhood. "You didn't mention other people being here," Archer said sourly.

"I needed Prudence, I mean I needed Pixie's help cleaning the blood up."

He looked down at me frowning, "What's she going to do, have her birds steal mops from the dollar store to help you clean?" he smirked at his own witty remark.

"No need to use the birds when I can just mop the floor up with you," she said from my window balcony. She jumped off the side slowly coming down to us.

As she finally touched the ground, I heard Rune from the window ledge say, "You know that gives me a heart attack every time you do that, right?" She looked up and blew him a kiss.

"Yeah, I have to agree with that," I said holding my chest. She threw her arms around me squeezing me tight.

"I am so glad you were not home when this happened," she said looking at the blood all over my face and back. Her face got red quick as she spun around and went toe to toe with Archer. "Did you do this to her!?" she demanded. Archer standing next to Pixie looked like a Great Dane standing next to a Yorkie. He was about to step up to her when Rune walked out.

"Is everyone ready to get this show on the road?" he asked. I nodded, as did Archer. Rune followed Pixie back into the building swatting her butt as she made it to the first step. "That's for jumping out of the window," he warned as she giggled.

We got upstairs, and as soon as Archer saw the bathroom, he asked me where a trash can was? Then excused himself to go throw up. The rest of us stood there at the door to the bathroom trying to come up with a game plan. "Archer can make the body vanish if he can focus long enough to do it without getting sick."

Rune looked surprised, "How can a fairy make people vanish?" he asked Pixie.

"I'm not a fairy, I'm a warlock," Archer said while putting a mint in his mouth.

"Hey, are those my mints!?" I asked getting upset.

He shrugged, "It's hard to say, I found them on the table in the kitchen."

Rune put his hands up to break up our argument. "So you guys are not like Pixie?" We shook our heads as he looked at Pix.

She gave him a smile, "I'm just a rare gem, my dear." She stood on her toes to kiss him.

"So!" I said breaking up that mush, "Like I was saying, Archer can make the body disappear if he doesn't keep getting sick." I looked to Archer who was holding his stomach.

He looked down at me. "It's not what you think, I have seen many dead bodies and worse than this even."

I turned to face him, "What's the problem then that is making you sick?"

He glanced at me, "The guy is just nasty looking, I would probably have thrown up walking past him if he was alive."

I smirked at that patting his back, "Well, nobody can blame ya there." Rune and Pixie nodded in agreement.

"After the body is gone, I can get some of my best guys in here to do the rest of the cleaning."

I looked at Rune, surprised. "How good are they?" I asked.

He gave me a sheepish grin as he spoke, "To be honest, most of them are from a high-security prison for murder charges."

Pixie looked up at him, "They must not be that good if they got caught, darling."

He looked down at her smiling, "They got caught because they went and told a pretty girl what they did." She giggled as Archer and I rolled our eyes.

"Great," I said clapping my hands together as I continued, "It sounds like they have good references for the job. Let's do this!"

Chapter Thirty-Seven

Within five hours all traces of Cleatus were gone. Archer stood at the street with me waiting for the Taxi. "You have Ellie's number, correct?" he asked while not looking at me.

"Yes," I replied looking up at him. "Thank you for helping me." He nodded still not looking at me.

He glanced down at my hand, "You can't use that ring forever. It's as bad as using a crutch with a bad leg. You need to build your own power up like I did."

I looked down touching the ring with my other hand. "Will you be able to work more with me?" I asked moving in front of him so he had to look at me.

"I probably will because Ellie likes you so damn much." He said finally looking down at me.

"Not that I care because you are still willing to train me, but is Ellie the only reason you are doing it?" He avoided looking at me again as he gazed up at the sky.

"No, I think you are a very powerful witch if you can get your shit in check," he let out a sigh before adding, "and I would rather keep you as an ally instead of an enemy."

I couldn't believe I got what I'm assuming is a compliment from him. He glanced over to me as I waddled over to him like a penguin hugging the side of him tight. "Awe

Archer, you really do love me!"

He snorted pushing me off of him, "Hardly."

His taxi rolled up to the curb and as he climbed in and as it began to drive away, I yelled, "I love you too, buddy."

Once he was out of sight, I went back into the apartment to see Rune and Ellie talking. I walked over to her and she hugged me, then remembering that I was covered in blood, dropped her arm. "You need to shower and change."

I looked at my bathtub and began to sniffle. "I know but I can't do it here anymore." Rune squeezed Pixie's shoulder and she smiled up at him.

"You are welcome to use our house until you can get a new one."

I looked at them both, "Thank you." He nodded and began to walk down the stairs to the limo.

Pixie grabbed me by the hand. "Do you want to just drive and meet us there if I give you the address?"

I shook my head, "I don't have a car anymore, Archer destroyed it, trying to destroy me." I looked at Pixie whose eye was twitching.

"That mother trucker," she said sounding angry.

"It's fine though," I said pulling the wad of cash from my pocket. "He reimbursed me for the damages."

She sighed and as we walked to the limo, she looked at Rune who had the door held open for her. "We need to stop and get Marcy a car, honey."

He looked at me then nodded, "We can get her two if you wish, my darling." She looked over and winked at me.

"No, I only need one car. Thank you, though." I replied handing him the cash I still had in my hands.

The limo dropped Pixie and me off at their house then Rune told us he would be back with my new car. We walked inside and I about died. "Pix, this place is huge!" I said admiring the enormous rooms, tall ceilings, and the beautiful tile floors. The walls were a light tan color. Pixie closed my mouth with her hand and giggled.

"Sorry for the mess," she said kicking her shoes off and walking up the stairs. I looked around at the spotless house.

"You know that angers me when clean people say that, right?" I said pulling my shoes (that's right, I got shoes now) off and following her.

She led me down a huge hallway to show me where her room was. Then she opened a door across the hall. "This is Horace and Milo's room," she said with delight as she opened the door and there were trees everywhere and the shell of a car with multiple antennas on it.

"Where are they at?" I asked looking in the trees.

She shrugged, "Probably downstairs stealing the silverware."

I looked at her with an eyebrow raised, "Doesn't Rune get mad?"

She giggled. "Sometimes, but he can't stay mad at me for more than 5 minutes," she said wiggling her hips causing me to laugh. We walked what seemed like forever until we reached the end of another hallway.

"Are you ready?" she asked with her hands on the door handles. I nodded watching her open the doors to the room I was going to stay in.

"It's beautiful, Pixie," I said in awe as I took it all in. The carpet was a light gray color with the walls a very light blue. As I walked in, I saw the white dresser and matching vanity.

I put my bag and the box on the dresser looking at the kingsize bed with silver covers and more pillows than I would probably ever use in my lifetime. I looked over to pixie who was standing at another door smiling. I walked over to her and opened the door to reveal a large bathroom with a bathtub as big as the king-size bed. I am not gonna lie I wept a little.

"It has jets too," Pixie said excitedly jumping up and down.

"Why wouldn't you and Rune make this your room?" I asked in disbelief.

She waved her hand at me, "Our room is much bigger than this, dear." I closed my eyes not even surprised to hear that.

"Thank you," I said turning to her.

She walked over to the closet to get some clothes picked out for me. "You're welcome, now get clean and throw those clothes away."

Chapter Thirty-Eight

Probably an hour or two later, I was stepping out of the bathroom wrapped up in a towel that I swear was made from Chinchillas, even though the tag on it said Egyptian cotton. I was in the middle of stuffing the other two towels from the bathroom in my bag when Pixie walked in. I froze looking at her then looking at the towels I had halfway in my bag. She, on the other hand, was grinning ear to ear with her arms crossed.

"Look, lady, this isn't a hotel you can swipe stuff from, and I can only have two crooks in my house and right now they are asleep on their car." After a moment she giggled. "I'm just kidding you can have them, there are more in the closet down the hall if you want."

I smiled, "Thanks, after I saw my aunt in my bathrobe, I had no other options."

She sat on my bed as I finished getting clothes on. "Rune has your car downstairs, he wants to know if you want it put in the garage but by the way you look, I'm taking it you are not staying." I was about to reply when my, "Jesus wants a hug!" chimed on my phone. She glanced over at it, "Is that the priest you made out with? Does he know that's his ring tone from you, cause while I think that's funny, it's kind of a jack ass move." I laughed sitting next to her to check my phone. My heart began to sink but I couldn't cry in front of Pixie, so I smiled at her. She read right through my BS as she asked. "What did he say?"

I sighed, "He said he got the call for his transfer, he leaves in the morning and wants me to meet him at the church shortly so he can say goodbye." I put the phone down looking at her. "I really like him, Pix, I don't know what I'm going to do."

She looked at me confused, laying back on the bed. "I thought you had a ring that will allow you to tango in the sheets with him and not blackout."

I laid back next to her laying my head on top of her stomach. "That's not the problem, Pix." I let out a sigh as she began to run her fingers through my hair. "I like him a lot and I feel selfish for liking him because I so badly want to ask him to stay but I feel like if I do that, I'm taking him away from his church and the people in it who need him more than me. It's his job, or his calling, or whatever the hell he calls it. But it seems like every time I try to stay away from him, something always happens to make us end up face to face again. So it hurts either way and I can't win."

"Well," she said after a moment. "What happens when you end up face to face with him?"

I looked up at her, "We have so much fun together, he's amazing in every way. We talk, we laugh, and we rock out to the same kind of music. He makes existing bearable." I sat up looking over at the dresser where the box sat. "It sucks because no matter what happens with us tonight, he is still leaving." A tear fell down my cheek onto my hand. I wiped my eyes feeling like a fool for crying over a guy. Pixie got up from the bed and walked over to the closet. After a moment, she emerged holding a very pretty knee-length off the shoulder emerald green dress.

"Then make tonight count," she said smiling.

Chapter Thirty-Nine

I came down the stairs entering the living room where Rune and Pixie were sitting together. "Does this look okay?" I asked feeling like the dress was too short in the back.

"Wow, you look great!" Pixie said standing up to get a better look.

"You nervous?" Rune asked smiling as he stood up next to Pixie.

"I'm a little sad because I know this is it," I admitted putting the white moon ring on my finger and checking to make sure that the black moon ring was still safely on a necklace around my neck.

"Just go and show him what he is going to miss," Pixie said wrapping her arms around Rune who told me that the keys to my car were next to my purse. I nodded giving them both a hug, Pixie touched the moonstone ring around my neck for a moment.

"Why are you wearing both, don't you only need the white one?" she asked looking at me.

I sighed before replying, "Tituba said the other one will be for someone in need and the black one is for starting over. I'm hoping he is the one she was referring to and this will keep him safe while he begins a new life." I felt like crying so

I turned around to leave so they wouldn't see how much my heart hurt.

Rune asked Pixie something in a low tone then I heard her tell him, "Oh, she's not, she never has underwear on. Honestly, I don't think she knows what they even are or owns any."

I turned around so fast feeling my face turn red. "Pixie! I do wear underwear; I was just running late this morning."

She laughed, "You are the definition of late, honey."

I shot her a glare then smiled, "True story." I turned around to leave, covering my backside with my hands as I walked away.

There were so many new cars in the driveway that I couldn't figure out which one was mine. I began to push the unlock button until I found lights flashing. I walked up to find a Lunar Silver Metallic colored Honda CRV Touring. "What the hell?" I asked staring at the car that cost more than $35,000.

I called Pixie's phone which rang twice before I heard, "Rune's mule barn. Head ass speaking!" I waited for her to stop giggling as I climbed in the car and turned it on.

"I did not give him that much money, why did he get this car?"

I heard fake static for a minute and, "Oh no, I'm going through a tunnel. Marcy, can you hear me?" Then she hung up.

"You lint licker!" I said looking at my phone with my eyes practically twitching from anger. I made a mental note to yell at them both later.

I began to head in the direction of the church, wondering what I would say to him, what he would say to me. A flash of lightning ran across the clouds and heavy rain followed. "Great," I said turning the windshield wipers on as the thunder roared a moment later. I sighed, wishing life didn't always hate me. "Really? I got all dressed up and even brushed my hair for once and now it decides to rain," I said looking up to the sky as another flash of lightning struck the ground somewhere up ahead because the thunder made a loud boom noise as soon as the lightning struck.

I arrived in front of the church pulling along the curb. Turning my car off I sent him a text, "I'm here." With no reply, after a few minutes, I got out looking at the large stained-glass windows of the church. It was beautiful in the dark, almost like a Gothic look. I let out a sigh taking in the smell of the rain. I began to walk up the steps to the front when I heard voices to the side of the building. Thinking, there was a side door to go in, I turned around and began to walk down the sidewalk to where the voices were coming from.

My heart was beginning to race faster and faster from being excited to see him. Then my stomach began to feel like it was climbing up my chest. I thought for a moment that was a weird thing but I dismissed that as just being nervous to finally get to do everything I wanted to with Ben tonight.

"You are just nervous, and it's okay," I said, giving myself a little pep talk. Lightning flashed across the sky and at that moment I got the feeling of déjà vu. That's a weird feeling to get, I thought to myself, then as reality began to sink in, I froze in place feeling the same panic and fear I had felt in my previous visions. My arms wrapped around my stomach to hold it in place as I stared in horror at the church. This can't be right, I thought falling to my knees.

"It must be another vision; it has to be another vision." I pleaded out loud to myself, as the rain began to fall down the stray strands of my hair onto my face. I stood up feeling like I was wasting precious time. I felt so ill as I looked around wondering what I should do. This wasn't just another vision I realized as I began to sob, this is my vision.

Chapter Forty

I can't believe I didn't realize this sooner, I thought, running to the side of the church hoping to hell that I was wrong. I was so wrapped up in my emotions that I didn't even put two and two together. As I entered the church's courtyard, I saw Ben tied to the stone table, stones of all sizes crushing him. There was no one else around that I could see, so I ran over to him.

"Ben, talk to me! Who did this to you?" I begged, looking into his eyes. He was mouthing words to me but over the rain and the thunder, I couldn't hear what he was saying. Blood began to come from his nose and mouth as he kept trying to tell me something.

"Oh Ben, I am so very sorry, darling." I wiped the tears rolling down his face, feeling like I was about to cry myself at his pain. "Don't talk anymore, I'm going to get you out of here, okay?"

I began to roll the larger stones from him to relieve the pressure. I got about four or five off of him as I heard footsteps then, "I just got your text." I spun around to see the cloaked figure. She looked exactly as she did in my visions, so pale with eyes so dark and a crazy look on her face.

"I don't know who you are but you messed with the wrong girl," I said walking in her direction.

"Not a step further, Marcy," she ordered raising one of the stones I just got off of Ben. I froze, afraid to break eye contact with her.

"What do you want? Whatever you want I will give you, just please let him go."

She gave me a wicked smile as she replied, "You can't give me anything. The only reason you are even involved in this is because you chose to love a monster." As she finished her sentence, she dropped her hand and I heard a horrible breaking noise and Ben let out a groan of agony. I turned around as the stone rolled off of his leg, it was now broken.

"NO!" I screamed angrily running towards the cloaked figure. She began to levitate multiple stones of every size throwing them in my direction. Each one passed through me as I finally reached her, lowering her hand with mine. I put all of my force behind me as I tackled her to the ground. I was on top of her, holding her cloak around her neck as tightly as I could. She began to gasp, then brought her hand up to claw at my face. I let out a scream of pain as the scratch was so deep on my cheek that blood began to fall onto her face. I brought my hand up to cover the wound which was my biggest mistake, as soon as I did, she thrust her body up, causing me to fall off of her. Once I was on my side, she wrapped her arms around my midsection from behind me, holding one of my arms to my side.

I struggled with everything I had in to get her off of me but nothing was working and I couldn't reach her. With my last effort of strength, I rolled onto my knees then threw myself backwards causing us to not only fall back but my head to crack on hers. We both groaned out in pain, holding our heads while lying next to each other.

"The action movies are a bunch of horse shit," I said with extreme pain in my voice. I got up on my hands and knees crawling over and falling on top of her hoping my fat was enough to hold her down.

"Let him go now!" I demanded, pushing her hands together against the ground.

"Not on your life," she breathed back, biting my arm. My arm hurt so much as I began to bleed from her bite, but I refused to let go of her hands. Out of panic, I leaned my head down and bit her ear as hard as I could. She shrieked out in pain as we both struggled with one another. I pulled my arm from her teeth and laid it across the side of her neck to push down with all of my might.

"Enough, you two!" shouted a voice, as lightning struck the tree in the courtyard causing a large branch to break with a loud crack, and crash to the ground near us. We both stopped and looked as my aunt Abby emerged from the shadows. She was dressed in a blood-red cloak, her hair was up in a bun with stray strands around her face from the rain. I felt a sense of relief that she wasn't hurt or dead like Cleatus. I was also relieved that she was here to help me.

Chapter Forty-One

"Aunt Abby, I am so glad you are okay," I said from where I was still holding down my opponent. She took a step forward still thirty feet away from us but near Ben.

"Of course I'm alright, why wouldn't I be?" she asked looking at me confused. I grunted as the girl under me began to move again.

"I was at my apartment and found Cleatus dead, I was afraid you were hurt." I saw rage go across her face for a moment as she looked at the body under mine.

"Yes, his death was unfortunate, and I really did enjoy his company, but his death is, as one would say, necessary for the good of the cause."

I felt the last bit of hope that I had fade away, as I realized what was going on. Hoping again that I was wrong, I asked, "What do you mean by that?"

She smiled, playing with Ben's hair as she looked at his pale face. "Exactly as it sounds," she said looking over to me.

I glared at her as she continued to pet Ben's head like he was a dog. "Aunt Abby, who am I laying on top of and why is she attacking me?"

She shook her head, laughing, still looking down at Ben. "My dear Marcy, that is your very own sister, Dorothy, that you are laying on top of, and she is only attacking you because you are protecting the wrong side," as she said that she slapped Ben across the face hard.

"Leave him alone," I screamed. She smiled at me, then resumed petting Ben's hair.

"That is no way to speak to your aunt who raised you." I felt pain in my arm as Dorothy dug her nails into my hand. I quickly repositioned my hands out of her reach.

I felt so confused and hurt at this moment staring down at her thin pale face. This was my sister that I have not seen in so long and wished almost every day that she was still in my life. On the other hand, she knows who I am and yet she is still trying to kill me.

"Oh, I wouldn't give her that much credit, Marcy." I looked away from her face to see my aunts. "She is merely a puppet in my play, I have controlled her since the day she left my house all those years ago. It wasn't hard either, since she was already broken from the Salem trials even at such a young age," my aunt went on taking a step away from Ben. "I was hoping since you were an infant that I could control you as well but for some reason, I could never break you in your dreams like I could Dorothy."

I looked down at my sister's face again, "Is she even aware that she is doing any of this?" I asked feeling a tear fall from my face as I stayed laying on top of her.

"She is not aware of what I am having her do. I control her thoughts, her feelings, and her powers. She is my weapon and even with a few minor hick-ups like Cleatus, she has worked very well for me over the years."

I looked at her shocked. "How long have you been killing all of these innocent men?"

She took a step towards me. "As long as you've been alive, and it's been so nice to build my group up over the years." She saw my look of disbelief as she laughed, "Oh yes, my dear, there are many, many more of us out there doing the same thing. We won't stop until all leaders of the church are dead."

I closed my eyes as another flash of lightning struck the roof of the church. I opened them back up to see my sister's face, she looked so ill and it broke my heart. I wished I could have been there for her, to help her get away from my aunt when I did. I had no idea. She could have started her life over with me in New York. That's it, I thought, hearing my aunt take another step towards us. Tituba told me to give the black moonstone to someone in need to start over and change their situation. I pushed more of my weight on my sister, mainly to cover what I was doing so my aunt couldn't see. I quickly broke the chain of my necklace, picking up the ring as it fell from the chain, I whispered to my sister, "I love you so much, Dorothy. I hope, with this power, you can free yourself from this torture." I put the ring on her finger as my aunt was now standing over me.

Chapter Forty-Two

I knew she was standing there, but I couldn't tell how much time it would take for the ring to help my sister. I squeezed her tight as I felt my aunt's hands grabbing my hair to pull me off of her. I yelled out in pain as I felt like I was being scalped. She threw me back, causing me to fall to the ground and roll away from them both near Ben. I tried to get up using the side of the stone table to help me. As I did, I pulled more rocks off of Ben looking over at my aunt who was now standing over my sister.

"Get up, Dorothy, we are not done here!" My sister didn't move and I began to worry that I must have hurt her badly. I managed to get his chest unburied from the stones, thankful that I could see it rising and falling telling me that he was still holding on.

"I know, darling, I'm trying to hurry," I said in a soothing tone as I started to uncover his stomach.

I was still watching my sister who remained on the ground causing my aunt to yell louder at her. "Get up, Dorothy, and finish this!" she kicked my sister causing her to moan out in pain, but not get up. "Don't just lay there, you useless little girl, get up!" my aunt shouted kicking her again. I looked at my progress and felt I had gotten enough weight off of Ben to go help Dorothy. I kissed his forehead then walked towards my aunt and sister.

"Stop this, Aunt Abby," I said with venom in my voice. She looked at me, about to reply when my sister began to get up.

"Finally, you decide to join us," my aunt said giving my sister one last kick for good measure as she said. "I suggest you do as I say a little quicker next time to prevent this."

I ran at my aunt when she told my sister to stop me. I saw more stones coming in my direction and as some went through me, one very large stone did not. It hit my stomach, knocking the wind out of me as I fell near the fallen branch. I sat there for a moment, desperately trying to breathe. My mind went into a panic, wondering if I was dying. Then after a moment, I realized a stone that size should have killed me and it didn't. I stood back up facing them both, my aunt looked unpleased that I got up.

"You just don't listen, do you?" she asked as she demanded my sister kill me first then Ben. "I was going to have you watch him die so you would think twice before choosing anyone to love again, but at this point, you are just as good to me dead as you are alive. You only have one power and that won't help me or the others with our mission."

I looked over at my sister and began to panic. She raised her hands to levitate the largest stone, the final stone that was meant for Ben and moved it to face me. It hovered in front of her but it didn't come flying towards me like in my vision. It was almost as if she was waiting for something, I looked at her face, realizing that she was struggling in herself. Was she trying to fight the evil in her that my aunt controls and just isn't strong enough? I took a step back and realized I had backed up to the wall of the church next to the tree. Fear fell over me as I looked around.

My aunt became impatient with my sister and screamed, "Throw the damn stone, Dorothy!" slapping my sister so hard as she did in my dreams. My sister didn't fall this time but it caused me to remember that it was my aunt who hurt her then, causing her to leave me. It was my aunt now, who was hurting everyone I love.

My aunt's expression was one of anger and rage as she stood in front of my sister's face to slap her again. "You are so useless, as soon as we are finished here, I am going to have you killed like I did your mother." As she raised her hand, I saw red. I could feel my body pulling all energy from the sky, the lightning was so strong inside of me, I was afraid I would break, but the hatred I felt for the woman who raised me was much stronger than the lightning.

"You had our mom killed?!" I screamed at her causing her to stop hurting my sister for a moment.

She spun around, taking a step forward, right where she needed to be. "Oh, did I forget to tell you that? Yes, I did, your mother became close with a man from the church. She told me he was a good man and he loved her even though she was a witch. Then, when she got pregnant with you, I knew it was his and I had to end her life before you were born. Unfortunately, the trials happened and I couldn't enter the town, so I made sure to put your mother's name and face in the fears of the towns people as they slept. Then when you both were brought to me, I realized you were still a witch. Your mother was already dead so I couldn't undo that. I just raised you both, hoping that once old enough, you would start off weak like your sister, and I could mold you into what I needed."

I saw my sister's expression turn from anger to pain as she was hearing my aunt's harsh words. I knew this had to end now. "Aunt Abby, you are a monster and I hope you die as painfully as everyone else you have killed in your lifetime." She laughed and it made my stomach hurt at how hollow it sounded.

"Is that right?" she asked.

I smirked, "You bet your ass it is." I felt all of the lightning I held within me leave as it hit her with such a force that my sister put her hands up to shield her eyes from the flash. My aunt fell to the ground at the same time the stone above her did. Thankfully, the noise of the lightning was so loud we didn't hear her lower body get crushed by the stone.

I ran over to my sister who was laying on the ground. I was afraid it hit her too by standing so close. "Dorothy, are you okay?" I held her in my arms as she lowered her hands to look at me.

"Marcy, I am so sorry, I had no idea," she began to cry.

"I know you didn't," I said, holding her close to me. We stood up and I began to walk to where Ben was to get the rest of the stones off of him. As I took a step, a hand grabbed my leg, causing me to scream. I looked down at my aunt who was bleeding from her mouth.

"Help me," she breathed, "I raised you."

I pulled my leg away, "I have to see a therapist because of the way you raised me, and I have the worst luck keeping one on a regular basis. But don't worry; I forgive you for messing me up. Though, I can't forgive you for messing up everyone else's life." She began to cough as I knelt down by her and whispered, "Take care." She reached for me again as life left her eyes. Her arm dropped to the ground with a thud.

I ran over to Ben and he wasn't looking any better than aunt Abby at this point. "Ben? Ben, can you hear me?" I choked out, feeling his wrist for a pulse. He barely had one and I began to panic. "Dorothy, help me, please," I shouted over to her crying. She ran over to the other side of the table and we began to get the rest of the stones off of him. Once they were off, his pulse wasn't any better and he was covered in cuts and bruises. His shattered leg was swollen and red. I called Pixie immediately to come and get Dorothy out of here.

"You will be safe there. I will see you when I'm done, okay?"

Dorothy wrapped her arms around me as I hugged her back. "I love you and I'm so sorry," she said with tears in her eyes.

"It wasn't you," I replied, "but we are going to get out of here and start over together, I promise."

Chapter Forty-Three

Pixie arrived, and once I convinced her that I was fine and that Dorothy wouldn't hurt anyone, she nodded and left with my sister. I called for an ambulance, but they told me that with the storm, trees were down all over the roads and it could take a while. I began to shake from fear that they wouldn't make it in time. I walked over to untie him from the table. He looked so pale that I was afraid he was going to die at any moment. Crying, I tried to sit him up a little to lay his head in my lap. He looked up at me and I smiled down at him running my fingers through his hair. He had blood coming from the sides of his mouth. I wiped them off and he grabbed my wrist, kissing it. "You can touch me?" he whispered questioningly.

"Yes, my love," I smiled, crying harder.

"Nice," he croaked out, swallowing hard, and then coughing. He closed his eyes and I heard sirens but they went right past us. I felt his energy fading away and I knew I was losing him. I felt so helpless as I sat there watching the man I love dying.

I looked behind me to the house he was staying in; if I could get him inside, he would be out of the rain and somewhere warm. "Ben?" His eyes were still shut and he wasn't moving. I shook him a little trying to bring him back to me. "Ben, sweetie, stay with me, okay. We need to get you to your house, can you help me get you there?" His eyes were still closed but he nodded. My heart was breaking with every second as doubt set in. He was so much taller than me, how on earth was I going to be able to help him walk with his leg broken? I sat him up more as I slid off the table first.

He opened his eyes and looked around. "Get that branch," he said pointing to the ground by the tree. I ran over grabbing the branch but it was too heavy that I couldn't get it over to him. "Well, it was a good try," Ben said sighing. I was out of options as I walked over and sat next to him on the table.

"You should lay back down," I said as I helped him lean back. He laid on his side and I asked him if his house was unlocked so I could go get him a blanket.

"Yes, there are spare blankets in the bedroom." He whispered.

Quickly, I made my way inside and grabbed a heavy blanket, going back out, I covered him. "Is that better?" I asked rubbing his back as gently as I could.

"I'm so cold." He said shivering, holding his hand out for me. I took his hand, holding it in mine.

"What can I do to help you?" I asked, kissing his hand.

"Will you lay with me for a little while, please?"

I smiled, "Of course I will." I got under the covers facing him as he wrapped me up in his arms. I was afraid I would hurt him but as I tried to make space between us, he only pulled me in closer.

I don't know how long we laid there together under the blanket but when I woke up the rain had stopped. I touched Ben's pale cheek, wishing I could do anything to help him. I tried a few times to get up and go get help, but each time I did,

Ben would wake up, looking into my eyes with fear in his own. "Marcy, don't leave," he said, his voice shaking from the cold and shock.

I began to cry, holding him closer in my arms as I whispered to him, "I promise, I'm not going anywhere." I knew I desperately needed to go get help but if I did and he died alone, I would never forgive myself. So much time had passed since I called for help, I thought, and no one has shown up. I was beginning to lose hope and worse than that, Ben was losing his too. "Ben, Ben!" I yelled shaking him. His eyes were not opening and he was barely breathing. I quickly sat up looking at him. "Ben, please come back," I begged loudly, shaking him harder until his chest began to move again. I collapsed back on to the table next to him, crying. "I have to do something," I said to myself getting up.

I ran into his house getting a large bowl and a washcloth. I began filling the bowl with hot water while grabbing another large blanket that was dry. I ran back out to the courtyard pulling the old wet blanket from him, I placed the new one on top of him making sure he was completely covered. I looked up to his face to see his eyes open, looking at me. He was mouthing my name over and over. My heart felt like it was shattering into a thousand pieces watching him suffer. I wiped his tears away while feeling my own fall. "I know, baby, I know," I said to him as I got back under the covers, lying next to him, I reached for the washcloth pulling it from water in the bowl sitting on the table above our heads.

"Please, let this work," I begged as I placed the wet cloth under the blankets, lifting up his shirt to put it on his stomach first where there was heavy bruising. I held it there, my eyes closed hard as I kept repeating, "Please work, please work, please work," to myself. After a few moments, I heard him let out a sigh. He looked like he was in less pain. Hoping it was working I quickly removed the rag, putting it back in the bowl of water. This time, I placed it on his chest, leaving it there until his breathing sounded better. I was shaking as I realized it was actually working. I got up from the table immediately, moving the bowl to the other end where his broken leg was. I pulled the cover back exposing the leg and bone. As soon as I put the cloth on his leg, I heard the sirens and saw flashing red lights on the sides of the church walls. "I never thought I would be so thankful to see police coming," I said laughing and crying at the same time. "Ben, you're going to be okay now," I smiled walking up to him and kissing his cheek.

As I turned to leave, he grabbed my hand causing me to turn around and face him. "Thank you," he said smiling.

I kissed his hand looking into his eyes ready to reply when I heard someone shout, "Over here, guys!" The emergency personnel were approaching, and I needed to get out of there quickly. The only place I could go without being seen was back in his house. I ran inside, standing at his kitchen window out of everyone's view, I watched carefully as the police and paramedics worked. Eventually, Ben was taken away on a stretcher and police were taking photos of the stones, the table, and my aunt's body. Once the scene was cleared and everyone had left, I felt like I couldn't stand anymore as I collapsed to the floor. I leaned my head against the cupboard now happy and thankful that it was all finally over.

Chapter Forty-Four

A few weeks had passed; spring was now here as Ben walked across the street with the assistance of a leg cast and a cane. He reached the corner where Marcy's shop, "Stems of Hope" was located. Looking up to the black and green sign, he smiled, adjusting the bouquet in his free hand. When he approached the two French doors, his smile instantly faded as he saw the bright orange sign that read, "Stems still available inside if you have a key and the combo to the safe, hope is all gone and so am I. For questions, comments, or concerns please don't call us, we'll call you!" It was signed at the bottom, "Love, Marcy Goode." He frowned reading the sign over again. There was a phone number listed under the writing that wasn't Marcy's but he thought he would try it anyway.

A female's voice answered, "Lost and Found Antiques, what may I find for you today?" He hesitated for a moment until she said, "Hello? I can hear you breathing."

He finally cleared his throat, saying, "Yes ma'am, my name is Ben Shepherd and I..." he was interrupted with a loud squeal from the other end that almost blew his eardrum.

"Ben, I am so glad you are calling, how are you feeling?"

He was confused as he answered, "I'm sorry, do I know you?"

She was quiet on the other end for a moment before replying. "Oh, yes, I'm sorry, how rude of me." She laughed as she continued on. "My name is Pixie, I'm Marcy's friend and I know you because I spent time in your hospital room with her while you were recovering."

"That's why I'm calling actually," he said once she was finished speaking. "I was needing to see Marcy before I left and her shop is closed. Do you know where I can find her?"

He heard her say thank you to someone before she was back on the phone talking to him. "I actually have a letter here at my shop that she asked me to give you, if you have time to come by." She gave him the address to the store and as they hung up, he got back to his car wondering what happened to Marcy's shop. Did she run out of money and couldn't afford to keep it open, he wondered as he drove the seven blocks to the "Lost and Found Antiques" store. Turning his car off and entering the store, he looked around until he located a tiny woman with blond short hair. She had her glasses on, staring at her computer with an earbud in one ear, staring at the screen. He didn't want to startle her since her door didn't have a bell like Marcy's shop did. He cleared his throat, causing her to look up and see him. She smiled, removing the earbud and walking over to where he was standing.

"Hello Ben, sorry, I didn't hear you come in, I was reading the paper from the day you were attacked. It's nice to see you awake and not in pain."

He gave a chuckle still not remembering her. "Yeah, well, I don't remember much about that night except Marcy saving me." She nodded then a few awkward moments passed before he asked, "So, you said Marcy had left me a letter. May I have it please?"

She looked around for a moment as though she couldn't remember where the letter was. "It's on its way, it should be here any moment," she said reassuringly as she smiled. He looked at her, wondering what she meant by that until she suddenly put her arm up and a large black crow flew in through an open window. He ducked, covering his head from the bird as it landed on her arm, dropping an envelope in her other hand. "Thank you, Milos, my love," she cooed at the bird as it squawked at her then flew away. She handed it to him saying, "One letter addressed to you, fresh from the bird's mouth." She laughed. He thanked her, turning around to leave. He was almost at the door until she said his name causing him to turn around and look at her.

"I don't know what that letter says but I just wanted to let you know that I have known Marcy a very long time and she has never let anyone else non-magical in her life until you. She talked very highly of you and cared so much about your safety. I know she wanted more with you, it just wasn't in her cards, unfortunately. I hope that helps you when you read that letter." He smiled before thanking her and leaving. He waited until he was in his car before opening the envelope and pulling the letter out. He closed his eyes letting out a deep sigh before opening the paper to read it.

"Dear Ben, I hope you are feeling better and more importantly, I hope you are having a good day today. I am sorry you have to read this letter instead of hearing it from me personally, but I had to leave as soon as possible. I wanted to explain to you why I left. On one hand, I love you more than I have ever loved anyone else before, but on the other hand, I know there are more witches like my aunt out there and you would always be in danger with me around. I couldn't live my life wondering when the next attack on your life would be. I never wanted to lose you and everything feels broken when you're not next to me. But it is better this way because I know you are safe. Please don't hate me for this." It was signed,

"Love always, Marcy."